In for a

Penny

The Whiskeys

MELISSA FOSTER

ISBN-13: 978-1948868617

Cover Design: Elizabeth Mackey Designs
Cover Photography: Wander Pedro Aguiar

WORLD LITERARY PRESS
PRINTED IN THE UNITED STATES OF AMERICA

A Note to Readers

If this novella is your first introduction to the Whiskeys series, each book is written to stand alone, so dive right in to this riveting love story and fall in love with Penny and Scott.

For avid fans of the Whiskeys, Penny and Scott have been two of my favorite supporting characters since I first met them earlier in the series, and I am thrilled to bring them to their happily ever after. I was taken by surprise, and quite delighted, when they came together in Quincy Gritt's book, THE GRITTY TRUTH. This story takes place several months after Quincy's book. I hope you love Penny and Scott as much as I do.

If you'd like to read more about the Whiskeys and Penny and Scott, I suggest starting with TRU BLUE, the first book in The Whiskeys: Dark Knights at Peaceful Harbor series.

You can download the Whiskey family tree here: www.MelissaFoster.com/Wicked-Whiskey-Family-Tree

See The Whiskeys: Dark Knights at Peaceful Harbor series here: www.MelissaFoster.com/TheWhiskeys

Remember to sign up for my newsletter to make sure you don't miss out on future Whiskey releases:
www.MelissaFoster.com/News

For more information about my fun and emotional sexy romances, all of which can be read as stand-alone novels or as part of the larger series, visit my website:
www.MelissaFoster.com

If you prefer sweet romance with no explicit scenes or graphic language, please try the Sweet with Heat series written under my pen name, Addison Cole. You'll find many great love stories with toned-down heat levels.

Happy reading!
~ Melissa

Chapter One

A WARM SUNNY day, a cool breeze coming off the water, and the hottest guy in Peaceful Harbor all to myself. What more could a girl want?

Penny Wilson opened her eyes, squinting against the sun at Scott Beckley, her boyfriend of almost seven months, lying beside her on the blanket on the deck of his small cruiser yacht, and she had her answer.

More.

With Scotty.

He turned his face toward her, catching her staring, and a wolfish grin curved his lips. His dark eyes slid down her body, lingering on her yellow bikini top so long her nipples pebbled. His eyes ignited, continuing their stroll down her body, visually devouring her, slowing again when he reached her bikini bottom, the muscles in his jaw bunching. *"Mm-mm.* Hello there, sexy," he said, rolling onto his side, giving her a glorious view of his six-plus feet of hard-bodied, work-with-his-hands ruggedness, *naked* save for his swim trunks.

His long fingers trailed down her belly, coming to rest on the edge of her bikini bottom, his palm searing her skin. He had the biggest, strongest hands she'd ever seen, and he knew just how to use them. Lust slithered through her core, coiling tight and hot beneath his touch. His eyes climbed slowly back to hers, full of wanton desire. She'd never met a more sexually potent man. From the moment they'd finally come together, they'd been combustible. His fingers curled around her hip, and he hauled her closer. He shifted over her, his hard length rubbing deliciously against her.

"You were too far away," he said in a deep, gravelly voice. "I like you better beneath me."

Scott was a man of few words, but he knew just how to use them to make her wet and wanting. He was a master at it, a giver and a *taker*. That was why Penny had gone on birth control, because she didn't want to delay gratification any more than he did. It was also why they never anchored too close to shore or other boats. They'd learned their lesson when they'd gotten carried away and were spotted in a compromising position by a passing boat full of rowdy twentysomethings.

She wound her arms around him, her heart beating so fast, she knew he felt it. "Why, Mr. Beckley, are you trying to seduce me on your *yacht*?"

Scott worked at the marina. He'd bought the old cruiser yacht for a song, and he'd spent the last year fixing it up, but he refused to call it by its proper name, referring to it as his *boat* instead. Penny didn't give a hoot about money or material things, but she cared about *Scott*. She wished he'd take credit for his hard work and how far he'd come from the teenage boy who had spent years protecting his two younger sisters from abusive parents. He had been kicked out at seventeen and had made his way in the world working on oil rigs as an underwater welder. His two younger sisters, Sarah and Josie, had later escaped on separate occasions from their parents' home in Florida using money Scott had left them. Unbeknownst to the others, Sarah and Josie had taken on new identities when they'd fled the state, and the three had lost touch. After a decade of looking, Scott had finally tracked them down almost two years ago and was now an integral part of their lives and a loving and protective uncle to their children.

Scott arched a brow, unwinding her arms from around his neck and pinning them above her head as he said, "Are you trying to get me riled up, Penelope Anne?" He pressed his warm lips to the swell of her breast. "Because you know how I get when you rile me up."

Oh *yes*, she did, and she freaking loved it. She arched beneath him as he kissed a path along her breastbone and sank his teeth into her other breast just hard enough to send spikes of pleasure rippling through her and draw a needy sound from her lungs.

"I was just calling your big-boy toy by its proper name," she said breathily.

"Funny. I didn't hear you say *cock*," he countered, using his teeth to drag her bikini top off her breast. He lowered his mouth over it, sucking hard.

She writhed beneath him, pleasure radiating down her limbs. His dirty talk had as much of an effect as the feel of his tongue and teeth, but it wasn't nearly enough. "If you're going to taste my sugar, you might as well enjoy my sweetest spot."

He ignored her suggestion, his dark eyes flicking hungrily up to hers as he lavished her other breast with the same scintillating attention. He rocked his hard length against her, bringing her every nerve to the surface. Her entire body vibrated with desire.

"*Scotty*," she panted out, trying to free her hands. "I need to touch you."

His serious eyes scanned the empty waters around them. For as much of a taker as he was, he *always* watched out for her, making sure she was not only on board with his actions but also safe.

In seconds he'd stripped them both naked, his eager erection reaching past his belly button. Penny's body pulsed with the need to feel him buried deep inside her, to be enveloped in his arms, to feel their love exploding between them.

She reached for him, but he shook his head, eyes dark as night as he lowered himself to his back and said, "I want *you* on my *mouth* and me *in* yours."

"Oh, you do, do you?" she teased, rising on her knees, loving the greed in his voice.

She'd never been shy about her sexuality, but she'd never

been with a guy she craved in the ways she craved Scott. When they'd first gotten together, he'd been *too* careful with her, tethering his desire to hold her tighter, flip her over, take a nip, or tug at her hair. She'd quickly waylaid his worries about hurting her, and now she loved taunting him.

"Hell *yes*," he said, like a curse.

He grabbed her hips, lifting her off the blanket and lowering her so she was straddling his face. With one yank, he had her exactly where he wanted her, and he took his fill, sending exquisite pleasure coursing through her. Her hips bucked as she rode his mouth, moans streaming from her lips. With the hot sun on her back, he worked his magic, turning her into a writhing, moaning, pleading bundle of raw nerves. She was utterly lost in him. When he put one hand on her back, gently pushing her torso down, she remembered what *else* he wanted and was more than happy to comply. She wrapped her hand around his length and took him into her mouth, earning a guttural moan. They drove each other wild, sucking, licking, using their teeth. She used all the tricks she'd learned he loved, like heightening his arousal by continuing to pleasure him even as her climax engulfed her. She felt his muscles go rigid seconds before he flipped her onto her back and came down over her, entering her in one hard thrust. His strong arms circled her, lifting and angling, all the while devouring her mouth and pounding into her. She fought against another orgasm, wanting to experience it *with* him. Everything was better with him. Her nails dug into his back as he stroked that secret spot inside her with mind-numbing precision. Prickles of heat climbed up her limbs, seared through her veins. Just as her control shattered, he gave in to his own powerful release, tearing his mouth away and gritting out her name through clenched teeth.

As they came down from their high, he cradled her in his arms, showering her with kisses, both of them breathless.

"*So* good, Pen. You fucking destroy me."

You make me feel whole.

She lay cocooned in his embrace, thinking about how far they'd come. She and Scott hung out with the same group of close-knit friends. This time last year, when Penny had attended a charity bachelor auction at Whiskey Bro's bar, that was all she and Scott had been—*friends*. The Whiskeys were like family to them, and Dixie Whiskey-Stone had put the auction together. It was a no-brainer that their single-guy friends would volunteer to be auctioned off, including Scott and Quincy Gritt, Penny's closest male friend. Almost everyone they knew had thought that Penny and Quincy would end up together.

But she and Quincy had always known better.

They'd become fast friends, but they'd never had the spine-tingling electricity between them that she and Scott had. The strange thing was, *Penny* hadn't even realized how much she'd liked Scott until the night of the auction, when he'd strutted his badass self onstage, drawing the attention of every woman in the place. Penny would never forget the tightening of her stomach or the jealousy that had clawed at her as she'd watched women bid on him. She'd thought about bidding on Scott, but he had never seemed interested in her in that way. He'd seemed interested in Cassie Lawrence, who owned the bakery down the street from Penny's ice cream shop. When Cassie had won the date with Scott, Penny had been shocked at how much it had bothered her. She'd been sure that Scott and Cassie would become an item, and that would be that.

But they hadn't.

And her secret attraction to him had simmered and sparked inside her every time she was around him. But he'd given her no indication that he was interested until last November when he'd been babysitting for his sister Sarah and her fiancé Wayne "Bones" Whiskey's three kids, Bradley, Lila, and Maggie Rose. Scott had called Penny asking if she would come help him with Maggie Rose, the baby. He'd sounded *different*, like a man who was interested in a woman, not just a buddy who needed help. The heat in his voice had gotten her all worked up. She'd done her best to play it cool, but after they'd put the kids to bed, he'd looked like a caged tiger, eyes blazing, restraint written in his taut muscles, and he'd practically growled, *Are you into Quincy?* His question had caught her off guard. Quincy had been hung up on his now-live-in girlfriend, Roni Wescott, for months, and she'd thought everyone knew it. When she'd said, *No, Scotty. I'm into you,* he'd hauled her into his arms and kissed the daylights out of her. And they'd been hot and heavy ever since.

"This is the life, isn't it? You and me, no responsibilities. Clothing *optional.*" He brushed a kiss over her lips and said, "We could sail away and disappear for a few weeks, just the two of us."

"That sounds wonderful." She gazed up at his handsome face, getting drawn into his fantasy. He'd changed a lot from the closed-off guy he'd been when they'd met almost two years ago. Even his appearance had changed. His hair had been longer, blonder, too. Cut short, it looked more like dark chocolate than caramel swirl. His eyes were more relaxed, less hooded. She was pretty sure shadows of his abusive parents would always be hiding in those gorgeous dark eyes, and she wished she could take those memories away. Scott had warmed to Penny and their friends fairly quickly, but he'd opened up to her even more once they'd come together, letting her into his tortured, loving heart. A few weeks at sea with that brave, loyal, delicious man who deserved everything good in life would be heaven on earth.

"There's nothing stopping us," he said.

"As enticing as that would be, that little ice cream shop of mine won't run itself." Penny owned Luscious Licks in her quaint hometown of Peaceful Harbor, Maryland.

"You hired three people for the summer. They can handle it."

He was right, they probably could. Penny had never needed permanent staff because she hadn't minded working long hours, and Quincy and Josie had helped out when she was overloaded. But this summer she'd wanted evenings and weekends free to spend with Scott. The two teens and one twenty-two-year-old she'd hired had come highly recommended and had been doing an excellent job. She knew Scott was only kidding, but the idea was so appealing, part of her wished he wasn't.

"I don't think Roni and Quincy would mind if we missed dinner at their house tomorrow night, but Sarah would be upset if you missed her wedding next weekend," she reminded him.

Penny couldn't be happier for Sarah and Bones. While Scott and Josie had found their way to better lives after leaving home, Sarah had ended up in the hands of another abuser. When she and Bones had met, she'd had two young children and was pregnant with her third. Bones had fallen hard for Sarah and her children. He wanted to give Sarah the wedding she deserved, and he'd gone all out, booking the elegant Davenport Estate, forty-five minutes outside of Peaceful Harbor.

The wedding would be bittersweet for Penny. She'd watched her older sister, Finlay, and most of their friends fall in love, and just as it had for her with Scott, love had come fast. But while the rest of her friends had moved forward and were living together, getting engaged or married, and having babies, she was living out of one drawer in his house, shuffling clothes back and forth from her apartment above her ice cream shop, even though they were together every night. She wanted to tell him how much she loved him, but he hadn't said those three magical words that took a couple to the next level to her yet. She didn't want to say it first and put her heart on the line. Who was she kidding? Her heart was already on the line. But saying it first would make her feel more vulnerable, and every time she thought about *why* he hadn't said it, which was a lot more often lately, she felt nauseous. She *knew* Scott loved her. She saw it in his eyes and felt it in everything he did. Even the way he was caressing her stomach right now was loving. But for a girl who wanted a family and a guy who didn't, love might not be enough.

Scott rose on one elbow. "I am looking forward to seeing you in that sexy little dress you bought." His eyes trailed down her body. "And to stripping it off you at the end of the night."

Goose bumps chased up her skin.

He trailed his fingers around her nipples, bringing them to hard peaks, and his eyes heated. "It's good to see you're looking forward to that, too."

God, she loved the things he said to her. "Who me?" She laughed softly. "I can't wait to see you in your tux, walking Sarah down the aisle, and to hear them say their vows. They're so in love. Aren't you excited about the wedding itself?"

"Sure. I'm happy for Sarah. All I've ever wanted was for her and Josie to be safe and happy. With Bones and Jed, I know they'll always be well cared for." Josie had married Jed Moon in February in an intimate gathering at Bones and Sarah's house, where they'd first set eyes on each other. Their seven-year-old son, Hail, had been the ring bearer.

"You'll never have to worry about that again with the Whiskeys and the rest of our friends around," Penny said.

"That's true." He brushed a kiss to her lips and said, "I have a surprise for you."

"Is it anything like the surprise you just gave me? Because I don't know if I can survive another yet."

He chuckled. "You're going to love this one. You know the dessert festival at Echo Beach?" Echo Beach was about an hour away from Peaceful Harbor.

"You *know* I do." She'd told him all about the Sweet 'n Savory Dessert Festival, which took place three times a year, each time in a different part of the country. Being an exhibitor in the festival was so sought after, it was almost impossible to get a spot. Participants were hand-selected. Penny was always trying to increase visibility for her ice cream shop and offer new things for customers. She'd applied as a participant to the festival several times but had yet to be accepted. "I told you I've wanted to go for the last three years and I haven't gotten accepted. I can't even score tickets. They sell out—"

"In less than three hours," he said, parroting what she'd told him months ago. "This year it sold out in *two*, but guess who's got tickets?"

Penny sat up in disbelief. "You do not!"

He laughed. "*We* do, sweets. That's where we're heading right after we shower."

She squealed and threw her arms around him, kissing him hard. "Thank you!" *IloveyouIloveyouIloveyou!* "You're amazing. How did you get them?"

"Maybe you can seduce that answer out of me in the shower." He stood up and helped her to her feet, keeping her close as they headed into the cabin.

With the early summer breeze at her back, a heart so full it bubbled over, and the man she adored kissing her lips, she could *almost* forget that their future stars were not aligned.

Chapter Two

ECHO BEACH WAS a charming seaside town with rows of brightly colored vintage cottages overlooking pristine beaches, and in the summers, a beachside Ferris wheel, a kiddie roller coaster, and a merry-go-round graced the waterfront. Scott had been to Echo Beach only once for a brief meeting. He was looking forward to exploring the town with Penny after they enjoyed the festival.

The festival was in full swing. Strings of lights crisscrossed over rows of white canopies on the crowded pier, each one boasting a different dessert vendor. A band was playing on a stage at the far end of the pier, competing with noise from the kid-friendly rides and the surrounding grounds, which were bustling with families, food trucks, and a juggling clown.

Penny pulled Scott through the crowds, smiling brightly and talking animatedly as they made their way from one exhibit to the next, tasting desserts from all over the country. He'd been drawn to Penny's carefree nature and snarky sass from the very moment they'd met. As he'd gotten to know her better, he'd realized she was also one hell of a businesswoman, always focused on what she could do better, what else she could offer to her customers. He loved her business prowess just as much as he adored everything else about her, from her enthusiasm for life and her caring nature to the way their mouths and bodies fit together so perfectly.

"This is giving me so many ideas!" she exclaimed as they walked away from a booth. "I've never thought about putting salted-caramel *popcorn* on ice cream. It's the perfect topping. Sweet and salty are always good together, and it adds a bite of crunch. I can put my own twist on it using peach or strawberry ice cream, and instead of caramel, use another flavor. I wish I had my notebook. I really need to write this down. There's so *much* here, I'm liable to forget half of what I think up."

"I've got it, babe." He whipped out his phone, typing as he said, "Salted-caramel popcorn on some other flavor like peach or strawberry. What else?"

"The ice cream pizza! I bet that'd be a hit with teenagers. And I want to try making coconut strawberry and coconut pineapple ice cream. Oh, *look!* Sweetie Pie Bakery. *Yum!* We have to go there."

She was so damn cute, bouncing from one booth to the next in those sexy cutoffs, her eyes dancing with delight. They tasted pies, cakes, cookies, tarts, and just about every type of dessert under the sun, and she rattled off ideas after nearly every one of them. Her happiness made him feel things that had boggled him at first. He hadn't thought anything could make him happier than knowing his sisters were safe and building better lives. But Penny's happiness had become his own. Loving her and taking care of her fulfilled him like nothing else ever had.

If only he could give her what she really wanted.

"Open up," Penny said, holding up a forkful of butter pecan bread pudding with cream cheese glaze.

She fed it to him and then she ate a bite, moaning like it was the best thing she'd ever tasted. That sinful sound brought his lips to hers in a long, sensual kiss.

He kept her close, whispering, "There is absolutely nothing on this planet sweeter than you."

She sighed, gazing up at him with a dreamy expression he'd come to love. Her light-brown hair flowed sexily over her shoulders. She was always gorgeous, even when she wore her hair pinned up in a messy bun secured with a straw or a pencil speared through it and one of the dozens of tiny colorful clips she hoarded. But today, with the sheen of a fresh tan and a navy tank top that made her big blue eyes stand out, she was even more stunning. Or maybe it had nothing to do with that tan or her clothes and everything to do with how big a part of his life she'd become. He often found those little hair clips in his couch cushions, and it made him happy every damn time.

A fucking hair clip.

He chuckled at the thought.

"What are you thinking about?" she asked.

As she came back into focus, he realized they were standing

in the middle of the walkway with dozens of people maneuvering around them. He got caught up in her so easily, he was used to the rest of the world fading away. She had become the voice that calmed and centered him, which he hadn't even realized he'd needed. The fact that he had never slept through the night before her should have clued him in. When they'd first started seeing each other, he wouldn't spend the night with her because he was such a fitful sleeper. But one night she'd told him how much she'd missed him when he left each evening. She'd said it had started to make her feel like their lovemaking wasn't as special to him as it had felt to her. She was honest like that about everything, and he'd confided in her about sleeping with one ear open because of the abuse he'd endured and said he didn't want to keep her up. The truth was, he'd slept even worse during their time apart. He'd stay up at night worrying about Penny, alone in her apartment.

He'd never forget the depth of emotions he'd seen in her eyes and had heard in her voice when she'd said, *I'd rather sleep an hour a night in your arms than several without you.* No part of him had wanted to deny her—or himself—and though it had taken some getting used to, she'd never complained about his initial restlessness. They'd quickly realized that he slept better at his house than in her apartment. He liked being in control of his surroundings, which stemmed from the way his father's temper could ignite at any moment, often in the middle of the night.

Scott knew the sounds of his house settling, the creaks

caused by wind, and even the feel and sound of the silence. Penny didn't mind staying at his house. The more nights they'd spent together, the less fitfully he'd slept, which had brought another revelation. As long as Penny was in his arms, he knew she was safe, and that had calmed another part of him. Now, as long as she was safely by his side, he slept deeply.

He gazed into her beautiful eyes and said, "You, sweets. *Always* you."

He pressed his lips to hers, and they spent the next few hours talking with vendors, jotting down ideas for her shop, and having a blast. Later in the afternoon, they shared a burger from a food truck on the grounds near the rides.

"This brings back so many good memories," Penny said as they strolled past the kiddie roller coaster. "My parents took us to the summer festival in Peaceful Harbor every year, and we always rode the Ferris wheel."

He pulled her tighter against his side and kissed the top of her head. She'd told him about her idyllic childhood. Her father had celebrated all of hers and Finlay's milestones with gifts wrapped up in big pink bows, and her mother had fed their passions, teaching Finlay to cook and Penny to make home-made ice cream and other desserts.

"I've never been on a Ferris wheel. Let's take a ride."

Her eyes lit up, and in the next breath, they saddened. "I know your childhood was horrible, but was it *ever* not as bad? When you were much younger? Four? Five?"

"Nope," he said, and headed for the Ferris wheel.

He'd hated telling her about the horrors of his youth. She'd cried for him and his sisters, breaking his heart anew. But she'd needed to know who she was getting involved with, because while she'd grown up with cotton candy and bubble gum, he'd gotten belts and bruises. He'd been up front with her about everything, and he'd told her that he wasn't looking for a wife or planning on having a family of his own. He loved his nieces and nephews to the ends of the earth, and he had never hurt a woman or child, or a man who hadn't been either causing someone else harm or threatening him. But he feared that his parents' abusive patterns might be lurking deep inside him, etched into his DNA, and he wasn't going to saddle any woman with a ticking time bomb like that.

The trouble was, he hadn't anticipated falling in love with her.

"You know we have to kiss at the top of the Ferris wheel," she said as they took their place in line.

He gathered her in his arms. "Is that a rule?"

"It's a legend of a curse. If a couple sits on the Ferris wheel, they're destined to break up. But if they kiss when it reaches the highest point, the curse is broken, and they'll be together forever."

"Forever, huh?"

He'd tried to convince himself more than once that he was being selfish by staying with Penny when he couldn't give her the family she wanted and deserved. He'd told himself he needed to end things with her, but he just couldn't do it. He loved her so damn much, he wished he was the type of person who could push past their issues and move forward more freely, like his buddy Quincy, who had overcome years of substance abuse.

Or Sarah.

His chest constricted thinking of the sister who had suffered as much abuse as he had. She'd left home soon after he did, only to fall into the hands of another abuser. Thank God she'd escaped him and was marrying a good man who adored her and her children. He had no idea why his parents had never abused Josie, but he thanked God every day she'd escaped their wrath. Although Josie hadn't gone unscathed. She carried heaps of guilt for having an easier time of it than they'd had. At least she'd ended up with a kind and generous young man who had gotten her away from their parents when she was thirteen and eventually had become her loving husband. She'd lost him too quickly to an undiagnosed medical condition, which was heartbreaking, but at least now she was happy and safe once again and married to a good man.

"That's right," Penny said with a hint of challenge, and pressed a kiss to the center of his chest. *"Forever."*

She was always challenging him, and he really dug that about her, too. But she never challenged him about his choice not to have children. She acted like she was cool with not having a ring on her finger or making plans for a family, but he knew her too well. He'd seen her with her niece, Tallulah, and his nieces and nephews, for whom they often babysat, and it always brought conflicting emotions for both of them. She was a natural with children, and she'd be an amazing mother one day. Which was why the fact that he was going to kiss her the *whole* time they were on the Ferris wheel to earn as much of forever as he possibly could probably made him a dick.

But there were far worse sins than loving someone too much.

THE TOWN OF Echo Beach was even more charming than Scott had remembered, with painted brick-front shops, old-fashioned streetlamps, and flower boxes bursting with gorgeous blooms. The street names—Peony Way, Daffodil Drive, Black-Eyed Susan Lane—followed the same floral theme as the garden and park, which anchored either end of the main drag, Bluebell Gardens and Primrose Park.

As they explored the shops, they picked up a cute mermaid rattle for Tallulah and gifts for each of Scott's nieces and nephews. They bought a truck whistle for Hail, a toy motorcycle for Bradley, who at five wanted replicas of everything his daddy had, a xylophone for two-and-a-half-year-old Lila, and a stuffed kitty for Maggie Rose, who was fifteen months.

They spent hours looking around, and as they were leaving an eclectic shop with everything from clothing to knickknacks, Scott caught sight of a small oval sign with green lettering that read LIFE IS BETTER WITH SWEETS, bordered by tiny ice cream cones with ice cream dribbling down their sides.

"Hold on, sweets." He picked up the sign and said, "We need this."

She laughed.

He slipped his arm around her, tugging her against him, and feigned a serious tone. "Did you just laugh at my choice of signs?"

"Yes, but only because I love it so much."

Not nearly as much as I love you. It pained him to hold back that declaration, but it wouldn't be fair to give it wings. Instead, he kissed her, pouring the passion he felt into their connection.

They bought the sign and then headed down the street to the Blue Fin restaurant where Scott had secretly made reservations. He had another surprise in store for Penny, and he knew her well enough to realize that if he'd told her what it was ahead of time, she'd have been a nervous wreck all day. He'd wanted her to enjoy every minute of the festival.

When they arrived at the restaurant, he said, "This looks perfect."

"I heard a couple talking about this place at the festival. I think we need reservations."

"Don't I always take care of you?" He'd researched the restaurants in the area to find one that had excellent food and service but allowed casual attire. The Blue Fin was noted as the best in casual dining. He opened the door and waved her in. "After you, gorgeous."

He took her hand as they followed a hostess through the restaurant to the back patio with a beautiful water view.

Penny whispered, "I can't believe you got tickets to the festival *and* made reservations here. You thought of everything."

"Because you are my everything," he whispered back.

He spotted his surprise, Alyssa Braden, a tall, dimple-cheeked brunette and the director of the Sweet 'n Savory Dessert Festival, waving from her table on the far side of the patio.

"Old girlfriend?" Penny teased.

"Hardly," he said with a laugh.

She knew that wasn't the case. He'd explained early on in their relationship that after leaving his hometown in Florida, he'd kept personal connections to a minimum to avoid having to answer too many questions about his past and to allow him to use his free time searching for his sisters. When he and Sarah had first reconnected after a decade apart and moved to the Harbor, they'd been on their way home from a celebratory dinner and had gotten into a horrible car accident. Bullet Whiskey had been the one to pull them from the wreckage, which was how they'd met him and his family. Sarah had been pregnant at the time, and she'd come out of it with scratches and bruises but thankfully, no major injuries. Lila had suffered a minor head injury, along with cuts and bruises. Bradley, luckily, had come away with only a few scrapes. Scott had gotten the worst of it with a broken leg, his other femur shattered, and a collapsed lung. While he was in the hospital, he'd developed an embolism and was in ICU. He'd had a long recovery and was left with a permanent plate and pins in one leg, along with a slight limp. He'd been focusing on recovering, physical therapy, and taking care of Sarah and her children, who had lived with him, when he'd met Penny. He'd also thought Quincy had been interested in her and had respectfully kept his distance. Not long after Sarah and the kids moved in with Bones, he'd reconnected with Josie. They'd moved into his house, and he'd cared for her and Hail, too.

Penny had never been far from his thoughts or his desires. While he'd hooked up with a couple of women, he'd *thought* that having a girlfriend wasn't even on his radar. But now he knew that wasn't quite true. He and Penny were together often during that time, as they hung out with the same group of friends, and over those months his feelings for her had deepened, obliterating even the desire to *look* at another woman.

"Scotty, why is she taking us to that woman's table?" Penny whispered.

"Because we're having dinner with her," he said.

Her eyes bloomed wide. "*What?* Why?"

He winked at the same time the hostess stopped walking and said, "Here you are," and motioned for them to walk past her to Alyssa's table. "Your waiter will be by momentarily."

"Thank you," Scott said as Alyssa pushed to her feet.

Before he could get another word out, Alyssa said, "It's a pleasure to see you again, Mr. Beckley." She offered her hand to Penny and said, "You must be Penny. I'm Alyssa Braden, the director of the Sweet 'n Savory Dessert Festival. Your relent-less—and clever—boyfriend has been singing your praises for weeks."

"Alyssa…" Penny said with disbelief as she shook her hand.

"Yes, Alyssa Braden," she repeated.

"I know who you are. I'm sorry. I'm just in shock," Penny said, flashing her killer smile. "It's a pleasure to meet you. Your parents founded the festival."

"That's right, sixteen years ago. You've done your home-work," Alyssa said.

"I've wanted to get into the festival for years. But I'm con-fused as to what's going on." Penny glanced curiously at Scott and said, "Scott *contacted* you?"

"I did. Why don't we sit down and I'll explain," Scott said as he pulled out her chair and they sat down. "Some businesses look great on paper. But you *are* your business, Pen, and Alyssa was kind enough to grant us an hour so she can make her own assessment about allowing Luscious Licks into the festival."

Penny's cheeks pinked up as she whispered, "*Scotty!*"

Alyssa chuckled. "Don't be embarrassed. You have quite a guy by your side."

"Yes, I do," she said, taking his hand under the table and squeezing it tight.

"Scott didn't just contact me, Penny. He called my office every day for two weeks and sent daily emails praising you, complete with descriptions of your special mood-driven sundaes and the other unique items you create. He also sent a slew of recommendations and quotes from other Peaceful Harbor business owners and residents. And when I didn't immediately respond, he printed them all out and overnighted them to my office."

"Oh my gosh. I'm so sorry," Penny said, giving Scott an incredulous look.

"Don't be. It's not often someone believes that strongly not only in someone else's expertise but also in the personality of that person. I'm looking forward to getting to know you to see if the woman behind the business lives up to all the hype."

Penny inhaled a deep breath, that incredulous look turning grateful, as she sat up taller, lifted her chin, and said, "I assure you, I do."

Now, there was the Penny he knew and loved.

Penny launched into a detailed explanation of how she'd learned to make ice cream as a child and had made it for all her friends and classmates. "When I was ten, my parents paid for my first booth at a community parade so I could sell my ice cream. That was the year I began making special flavors and sundaes based on people's moods…"

Penny had told Scott those stories, and still he was as captivated by her as Alyssa appeared to be. Over dinner, Penny talked about how Luscious Licks had come to be after her father had passed away almost four years ago and her mother had allowed her and Finlay to use the life insurance money to open their businesses.

Much later, as they left the restaurant, Alyssa said, "I'm

impressed with your personalized approach and your passion for your business, and I am thrilled that Scott persevered. Penny, you are *exactly* the type of person we want at our festival. You can look forward to an invitation to exhibit at next year's festival."

Penny gasped, and her hand flew over her heart. "*Really?* Oh my gosh, thank you! Thank you so much!"

She turned that elated smile on Scott, and he wished he could take her into his arms and spin her around and tell the world how proud of her he was. "Congratulations, sweetheart."

"I am curious about something," Alyssa said with a serious expression. "Scott reached out to me after talking with Ace and Maisy, my relatives who own Mr. B's microbrewery in Peaceful Harbor. I made a few calls, and I understand that you know several of my cousins from the Harbor and from Pleasant Hill, Maryland. Jillian said you make her wonderful sundaes after she has bad dates, and Tempest said she brings her little boy, Philip, to see you all the time, and you make sundaes for him on the spot. Since it's clear that you did your homework on the festival, Penny, I'm sure you realized that I was related to your friends. Why didn't you use your connections to reach out to me?"

"Because I didn't think that was fair," Penny said earnestly. "I wanted to be accepted on merit."

"I can assure you that no one gets accepted into our festival on anything other than merit. But use your connections, Penny. In this busy world we live in, it's hard to stand out among crowds. The more friends and colleagues we have, the better."

Alyssa shifted her attention to Scott and said, "You were right, Scott. Paper does not do Penny justice. Thank you for bringing her to my attention."

They talked for a few more minutes, and then they said their goodbyes. After Alyssa had driven away, Penny let out a squeal and leaped into Scott's arms, exclaiming, "I love y—that you did this for me! Thank you!"

His chest constricted as he spun her around. She had stumbled over those three special words a lot lately. As he pressed his lips to hers, he knew he'd been a fool to think kissing on a Ferris wheel could keep this extraordinary woman who had so much love to give she overflowed with it by his side forever.

Chapter Three

"DO YOU KNOW that this is one of my magical flavors?" Penny asked a towheaded boy Wednesday midmorning as she handed him a single scoop of rainbow sherbet in one of the kiddie-sized chocolate-dipped gingerbread cones that Josie made for the shop each week. Penny loved giving kids a little something extra, and after checking with the boy's mother, she'd put chunks of chocolate and gold flakes in the bottom of his cone.

He shook his head and licked his sherbet.

Penny crouched before him and said, "When you get to the bottom of your cone, if you find chocolate or gold, it means you're going to have good luck for a *whole* month. If you find both, you'll have good luck *forever*."

His eyes widened. "I hope I find them!"

"I hope you do, too," Penny said, sharing a smile with the little boy's mother and with Finlay, who had stopped by to show Penny the frilly pink dress she'd bought for her four-month-old daughter, Tallulah, to wear to Bones and Sarah's wedding.

Penny rang up the customer's purchase, and as she handed the boy's mother her change, she said, "Enjoy your afternoon." After they left, Penny wiped down the counter, watching Finlay lean into the stroller, talking softly to Tallulah.

"Thank you again for the rattle, Pen. Lulu loves it." Finlay shook the mermaid rattle Penny and Scott had bought for Tallulah at Echo Beach.

Usually being at the shop or hanging out with her sister brightened any mood Penny might be in. But it had been three days since she and Scott had had dinner with Quincy and Roni, and Penny hadn't been able to shake the green-eyed monster that had been perched on her shoulder ever since. She *hated* feeling jealous when Scott was an amazing boyfriend. But if he couldn't even say he loved her, then where did that leave them?

"I'm glad." Penny set down her rag and tried to push away her thoughts as she went to join them at the table, focusing instead on how fantastic her weekend had been. She'd raved to Finlay when she'd first come in about what Scott had done for her, just as she had to Quincy and Roni on Sunday. They were all as elated as Penny was. "I still can't get over Scott reaching out to Alyssa. He's such a private guy. He doesn't even like to ask for help, much less ask for favors."

"But he loves you, Pen, and love does crazy things, as we know by the fact that my husband told Kennedy she could name Lulu. Not that I mind. I adore her name." Finlay was married to Bullet Whiskey.

"Bullet also lets Kennedy put bows in his hair," Penny said with a laugh. Kennedy was Quincy's precocious five-year-old sister-turned-niece.

Kennedy and her three-year-old brother, Lincoln, were Quincy's much younger siblings. Their mother was a drug addict. She'd overdosed a few years ago, and their older brother, Truman, and his wife, Gemma, were raising Kennedy and Lincoln as their own children.

"Remember Halloween two years ago? All the guys wore cheerleading costumes because Kennedy asked them to so she could be a football player. All those hairy legs!" Finlay laughed so hard Tallulah startled and whimpered. "I'm sorry, baby girl. Come to Mama."

"Let me hold her," Penny said, nudging Finlay out of the way and lifting Tallulah into her arms. Tallulah was beautiful, with a mop of Bullet's thick dark hair and Finlay's blue eyes.

Penny nuzzled the baby's cheek, inhaling her sweet powdery scent as she took her seat across from Finlay. "Saturday was *the* most romantic day of my life, and not just because Scott went to such amazing lengths to hook me up with Alyssa Braden. Everything about it was wonderful."

Finlay leaned on the table, her blond hair framing her pretty face. "You say that every weekend."

"I know, but it's true. I *love* being with Scott. It doesn't matter if we're on the boat, making dinner, or just sitting together doing nothing more than holding hands." She tickled

Tallulah's belly, lighting up her pretty blue eyes. "I love his voice and the way he laughs." She wiggled the baby's foot, earning a sweet smile. "I love that he makes special time for his nieces and nephews, like I do for you, Lulu. Today he's taking Lila to the bookstore for story hour, and I know he's going to watch over her like a hawk. That's another thing I love about him. He's protective of the kids, of his sisters, and of me, which I know is nothing compared to how protective your hubby is of our little Lulu, but still." Finlay's husband, Bullet, was a tough biker and ex–Special Forces. He was also the most protective father she'd ever met. He'd carry that baby twenty-four-seven if he didn't have to work.

"Poor Lu is never going to be allowed to date. Red and I are already planning an intervention for when she's a teenager." Red Whiskey was Finlay's mother-in-law.

"Good luck getting the chastity belt off. Bullet will probably have Scotty weld it on. Right, Lulu?" She wiggled the baby's foot again. "Daddy is not going to let you have *any* fun."

Finlay laughed and ate her ice cream. After a few minutes, she said, "How was dinner with Quincy and Roni?"

"Fun, as always. We grilled out and sat around the fire pit talking. They're so supportive of each other. You should have heard Quincy raving about how good Roni's upcoming dance production is going to be." Roni taught dance at a studio in town, and she'd just started her own contemporary dance solo production company. Her first production was taking place later that summer. "I couldn't be happier for them. Or more jealous."

Finlay's brow furrowed. "Jealous? Of what?"

"Their five-year plan."

"*Oh*," Finlay said empathetically. "I guess that means you and Scott aren't any closer to saying *I love you* or moving in together?"

"Don't you think I would have called you and told you if we were?"

The door to the shop opened, and as if his ears were burning, Scott walked in with Lila in his arms. Penny's pulse quickened the way it did every time she saw him. She pushed to her feet with Tallulah in her arms and said, "Hi. I didn't expect to see you two before story time."

"I couldn't come into town and not stop by for a little sugar." Scott leaned in for a kiss and said, "My favorite flavor."

"You guys are too cute," Finlay said.

Scott winked at Penny, setting butterflies loose in her belly, and said, "She makes us cute."

"*Lulu!*" Lila reached for Tallulah, her little lips puckered. Penny stepped closer so Lila could kiss her cousin, and Lila exclaimed, "Kiss *you!*"

"You know I want super-special Lila kisses!" Penny said as Lila kissed her.

"Ice *ceam?*" Lila asked.

"You bet, Li." Scott set Lila down and took Tallulah from Penny, stealing another kiss in the process. He snuggled the baby and said, "How's our pretty girl?" as he sat down at the table with Finlay.

Penny took Lila's hand. "Let's go pick a flavor." *Before my ovaries explode.*

As she helped Lila choose a flavor, she heard Finlay say, "I hear you achieved boyfriend-of-the-year status last weekend."

Scott chuckled. "All I did was make a connection. Penny did the rest." He looked at her as she scooped ice cream and said, "I knew nobody could resist her charms."

How could she have been jealous of anyone else's relationship when she had the perfect man?

Penny must have asked herself that a dozen times as they chatted with Finlay and Lila ate her ice cream. Scott wiped Lila's spills and made her laugh and still fit in a few kisses and sexy glances for Penny.

When they got up to leave, Penny walked them to the door, and Scott said, "Want to go for a walk on the beach tonight?"

"Yes, that sounds wonderful."

Scott pressed his lips to hers, holding Lila's hand, and Lila made kissing noises at Penny.

Penny knelt to kiss her and said, "Have fun at story hour."

Lila nodded. "See Unca Kinsy."

"That's right, baby. We're going to see Uncle Quincy." Scott ruffled Lila's hair, then set a loving gaze on Penny and said, "Meet you here after work for our walk?"

"Sounds good." Penny locked the door behind them and hung up the sign that read THE ELVES ARE MAKING ICE CREAM. BACK IN 30 MINUTES and stalked behind the counter.

"You're closing?" Finlay asked as she began nursing Tallulah.

Penny scooped several types of ice cream into an enormous container and said, "I'm making an *I Suck* sundae." She piled on M&M's, chocolate flakes, granola, gummy bears, strawberries, smothered them in whipped cream, and flopped down at the table with Finlay. "Did you see how great he was with Lu and Lila? How much he adores me?" She sighed heavily. "I hate myself so much right now."

"Why?"

Penny shoveled ice cream into her mouth. "So many reasons."

"How about you start with one or two?"

"Well, for starters, we've been together for seven months, which feels like a long time because we're in so deep. But it's *only* seven months, Fin, not years, and he's been through so much. I don't want to pressure him, and I hate that I compare our relationship to anyone else's. But it's hard not to when all of our friends end up living together, engaged, or married in the blink of an eye. Bullet proposed to you after a month—"

"Thirty-five days," Finlay said.

"Seriously? Like those five days make a difference? Jace proposed to Dixie after what? Two weeks? Even Quincy and Roni moved in together fast. Love happens fast, and it did for us, too. But usually people fall so desperately in love they want *more* time with the other person."

"You and Scott are together every minute you're not working," Finlay pointed out.

"I know that. I'm not asking for more. I just…" Her stomach lurched. She pushed her sundae away. "I can't eat this. Every time I think about what our future looks like, it makes me feel like I'm going to barf."

"Know what else does that?" Finlay asked with a tease in her eyes. "Pregnancy."

"*Please.* You just want someone else to share in your sleepless nights. I'm on birth control, remember?"

"Mom got pregnant twice on birth control," Finlay reminded her. "You felt sick last week when we had lunch."

"We were talking about this then, too."

"True, but you two have sex *all* the time."

"Would you *stop*?" Penny laughed.

"Oh my gosh, Penny. You felt sick a few weeks ago when we all had dinner at Whiskey Bro's. Remember? You and Scott left early. How long have you been feeling sick?"

As Penny thought about the past few weeks, she realized she *had* felt nauseous a number of times. "Now you have me worried."

"I could be wrong. Take a pregnancy test. You'll know in five minutes if you're pregnant or just stressed."

"God, that's all I need. I can't even think about that possibility. I keep asking myself if Scott and I could just go on like this forever."

"Living together but not really living together?"

"Yeah. It sure feels like we could most of the time. I swear I fall deeper in love with him every day, with every touch, every kiss, and every conversation. Even the hard ones. When he came in here, I got butterflies. But if we just go on like this, will I look back on my life and wish we'd had children? Do you think our love is big enough to fill those empty places?"

Finlay brushed her hand over Tallulah's head and said, "You shouldn't ask a new mom that, because this little girl is everything to us."

"I know. I get that. I love him so much, I wish I didn't *want* children. I never even thought about having a family in any serious way until Scott and I got together. You've seen him with kids. He's as natural with them as we are."

"He's amazing with children, Pen. But that doesn't mean he should have his own if he really doesn't want them."

"I know. I think he *does* want kids, but he's scared. And people change their minds all the time. Look at Tru. He was fresh out of prison. He wasn't looking for a wife and two kids." She sighed, feeling like she was grasping at straws, and said, "Do you think I'm hoping for too much? I don't need a five-year plan. I just want a smidgen of hope that one day Scott will want more with me. I don't even care if our plan takes ten years, as long as I know he wants to eventually get there and that he's willing to work on it together."

"I don't think you're hoping for too much, but have you talked to him about all of this?" Finlay asked.

"We've talked about what we want plenty of times. He knows I want kids, and I know he doesn't want them. I feel *guilty* for even feeling this way. It's not fair of me to ask for more when I knew what I was getting into at the beginning of our relationship."

"Yes, but you didn't count on falling in love, and you probably thought if you both fell, he'd change his mind. That's only natural, Penny. I never thought Bullet would want to be monogamous, much less married with a baby."

"I know. I don't want to change *Scott*. I love who he is. I just want more of a future together. I want to live in the same place and know that one day we can have our own Lulu." As she said the words, she realized her mistake, and her stomach sank. "Oh my God, Fin. Trying to change Scott's mind about what he wants *is* trying to change him. I've turned into one of those awful girls who thinks it's okay to try to change her boyfriend, and I didn't even realize it."

PENNY SPENT THE next two days in a state of confusion, struggling with the guilt of wanting more of a future with Scott *and* mired down with worry over Finlay's pregnancy comments, which all made her even more nauseous. As bad as the days were, when evening rolled in and she was in Scott's loving arms, all her worries about the future fell away because their present was so wonderful. They laughed and loved and were *so* good together she tried her hardest to bury those other thoughts. But when morning came, her worries pressed in again, she felt sick, and on the heels of the nausea were Finlay's comments.

By Friday afternoon she couldn't stand it any longer. They were going to the rehearsal dinner in a few hours, but how could she think about anything in the future if she didn't know where she stood in the present? She closed the shop half an hour early and bought a darn pregnancy test. She couldn't imagine why the box had three tests in it. It seemed like overkill. Wouldn't two be enough? Did people really need tie breakers?

Now she was sitting on the side of the bathtub in her apartment above the ice cream shop watching the seconds tick by on her phone. Her hands were sweating, her nerves were buzzing, and her thoughts were spinning. After a minute, she was too anxious to sit still. She got up and snagged the test off the counter, staring at the tiny window as she paced.

A pink line appeared.

Negative.

Relief swept through her, and she tipped her face up and closed her eyes, exhaling a breath she hadn't realized she'd been holding. She put her hand to her chest, trying to calm herself down, and looked at the test again.

A second, fainter line appeared.

Penny squinted, taking a closer look, and grabbed the box, scanning the instructions. *Two lines. Pregnant.*

Oh my God.

She couldn't believe it. There was no way the test was right. She tore open another test and took it. When that one resulted in a positive, she opened the third one. Suddenly three didn't seem like enough. Her heart sprinted in her chest.

Positive.

I'm pregnant? Holy crap, I'm pregnant.

She sank down to the edge of the tub as unfamiliar sensations rained over her. Her skin went hot, then cold, bringing gasps and goose bumps, and a disbelieving laugh tumbled out. Her hand covered her heart as a happier, surprised "I'm pregnant" came out in a whisper. She placed her hand on her belly, an unexpected calm enveloping her. "I'm going to have a baby."

We're going to have a baby.

She froze as that sank in, and her hands began to tremble. Her throat thickened, making it hard to breathe. If Scott couldn't even say he loved her, then what hope did she have that he'd want this baby?

She sat frozen in place for a long time, *numb*, wanting to be happy but feeling devastated. She had to tell Scott, but she couldn't tell Scott tonight. Not before the rehearsal dinner and definitely not tomorrow before the wedding. It would be too stressful for both of them, and that wasn't fair to him or to Sarah. It was going to kill her to wait, but she had to. She'd tell him tomorrow night, after the wedding.

That decision made the pregnancy even more real. She swallowed hard as warring thoughts raced through her mind. *Maybe he'll be okay with it. What if he's not? Of course he won't be. He's afraid to have kids.*

Oh God.

I could lose Scott.

Our baby could lose its father.

She closed her eyes against a rush of tears as a ridiculous thought sailed through her mind. *If only Finlay didn't put the thought in my head, I wouldn't have taken the test.* The wave of guilt that followed made her nauseous again.

"I didn't mean it." She rubbed her belly, tears streaming down her cheeks. "I want you, baby. I just hope your daddy does, too."

Chapter Four

PENNY SLITHERED OUT from under Scott's arm Saturday morning, careful not to wake him as she stepped from the bed. They'd had a great time at the rehearsal dinner, celebrating with their friends. Sarah and Bones were so happy and in love, it gave Penny hope that maybe Scott would realize that acknowledging their love, getting married, and having a family wouldn't be so bad after all.

She pulled on one of his T-shirts on the way to the bathroom, walking past his tuxedo hanging on the closet door. She knew that when she saw him walking Sarah down the aisle, she'd have even more fantasies about walking down an aisle to him one day, just as she'd had at Josie's wedding. But now in that fantasy she imagined Scott holding their baby, beaming with pride.

She held on to that fantasy with everything she had, because any other was too sad to think about.

As she used the bathroom and brushed her teeth, she

thought about how many times she'd almost told Scott she was pregnant last night. She didn't even know how she was going to tell him after the wedding, when it wasn't fair to ask him to change, and she couldn't imagine a future without him. But she knew one thing for sure. Their baby was created out of love, and she wanted it as badly as she wanted him.

She headed down the hall to the kitchen, reminding herself not to think about any of it until after the wedding. She was determined to make today extra special for Scott for two reasons. First, because she knew he was nervous about walking Sarah down the aisle. When Josie and Jed had gotten married in February, it had been an emotional day for him. The second reason was for Penny as much as it was for Scott, because if he ended their relationship when he found out about the baby, at least they'd have these last few, hopefully magical, hours together.

She forced thoughts of the pregnancy down deep while she made blueberry-banana pancakes, and images of Scott's teary eyes as he'd walked Josie down the aisle tiptoed through her mind. He loved his sisters so deeply, he'd confided in her about feeling like he'd failed them when he'd been kicked out of their parents' house and had been unable to take them with him. Seeing all the good things he'd hoped Josie would one day find coming true had overwhelmed him. Penny knew it might be even harder for him with Sarah, since Sarah had suffered at the hands of their parents just as he had. That was why she was making Scott's favorite breakfast.

While everyone else was worried about making today perfect for Sarah and Bones, Penny was making it perfect for Scott.

She transferred the pancakes to plates, poured two cups of coffee, and put everything on a tray. As she carried it down the hall, it dawned on her that Scott had spoken of his hopes for his sisters' happiness many times, but he rarely spoke of the same for himself.

He was still fast asleep, so different from the restless sleeper he'd been months ago. She set the tray on the nightstand and took a moment to admire the incredibly loving, loyal man sleeping on his back with one arm still stretched across her side of the bed, the covers bunched around his waist. One leg peeked out of the blanket, the scars from his accident carving paths through his leg hair. She climbed onto the foot of the bed and kissed those scars. Then she kissed her way up his torso, tossing her own hopes for him up to the powers that be. Hopes that he wouldn't sell himself short and would one day see that he would be an incredible, loving father and husband. And then she tossed out one more hope. *If he truly doesn't want those things, then please help me get through the grief of losing him so I can raise our baby with all the love it deserves.*

"*Mm.* Mornin', sweetheart," he said in a groggy, sexy voice. He reached down, eyes closed, his fingers threading into her hair as she kissed the ridge of his pecs.

The adoration in his voice and his loving touch was all it took to push her thoughts aside and want to make love to him, to be as close as they could possibly be. She slicked her tongue over his nipple, and he pressed his hand on the back of her head, keeping her mouth there, another appreciative sound rumbling up his throat. She teased him the way she knew he loved, using her teeth and tongue, and his chest rose against her mouth.

"You feel so good, baby."

His hips thrust, his erection tenting the sheet. She loved the things he said, the effect she had on him, and Lord help her, she was falling even more in love with him right that very second. She felt it, a pull deep inside her, wanting to make today not just extra special but the best day of their lives.

"I brought you breakfast in bed," she said, tracing a muscle in his arm with her fingers.

"You're the only thing I'm hungry for."

He reached for her, but she wasn't done loving *him*, and she kissed a path lower, her lips playing over his abs as she stripped away the sheets. She wrapped her fingers around his hard length, intent on driving him wild. He thrust as she lowered her mouth, closing her lips around him, their eyes connecting with the heat of a thousand suns. He watched her stroking him slow and tight, sucking and licking, drawing sinful moans from his lungs.

"Don't come," she taunted, and took him to the back of her throat, quickening her efforts. His every muscle corded tight, eyes ravenous as she swirled her tongue around the head.

"I fucking love your mouth," he gritted out through clenched teeth.

It was a good thing her mouth was full, because *I fucking love you* was perched on the tip of her tongue. She drew away from his cock slowly, and he groaned. She grinned, whipping off her shirt as she straddled him and sank down, her body stretching to welcome every inch of his hard length. She stilled, her sex clenching. His eyes narrowed as he clutched her hips, trying to get her to ride him, but she loved teasing him too much and continued pulsing her inner muscles.

His eyes turned volcanic. "You've gotta *move*, baby."

"Not yet," she whispered, reached behind her and fondled his balls.

His hips shot up. "*Fucking* hell."

The desire in his voice sent lust coursing through her. She brought one hand to her breast, the other between her legs, earning even sexier, greedier sounds. His hips pistoned, his fingers digging into her flesh as he lifted her up and pulled her down with his every thrust, stroking over that titillating spot inside her at a feverish pace. Pleasure engulfed her, and she cried out his name. In one swift move, he shifted her onto her back and captured her mouth with his. She abandoned all control, and their bodies took over, falling into perfect sync, taking them to that magical place where nothing else existed. He loved her so exquisitely, she soared toward the clouds, enveloped in love so pure and all-consuming they felt like one being as they catapulted into ecstasy.

When they collapsed to the mattress, Scott gathered her in his arms, snuggling her entire body from feet to chest. She felt buffered from the world, and she never wanted to leave the safety of his arms.

"Feel that?" he whispered into her ear.

"Mm-hm. I always do when we're cocooned in our love." The second the *L* word left her lips, she cringed, thinking she should take it back. But she didn't *want* to, and she was too nervous to do anything more than lie there, eyes wide as saucers.

As the silence stretched from seconds to minutes, she was sure she'd made a huge mistake. The forbidden word churned between them, buffered in so many conflicting emotions, it made her heart ache. He shifted, and she feared her man of few words would get up and simply walk away. But one of his arms slid lower, his fingers spreading across her lower back. He gripped her shoulder with his other hand, holding their bodies flush from chest to thigh, as if he were trapping the word between them and was never going to let it—or *her*—go.

She closed her eyes, hoping he never would.

AN HOUR AND a half later, they were rushing around getting ready. They'd fallen back to sleep and had bolted out of bed in a panic. They had to leave in twenty minutes, or they'd be late for the wedding.

Penny finished drying her hair and shoved her hair dryer beneath the sink, hurrying out to the bedroom in her towel to grab the sexy lingerie she'd bought to match her dress. As she dug through her bag, she pulled out her heels and realized she'd brought an unmatched pair. "*Shit!* I brought two different heels." She looked at Scott, who was pulling on his slacks, and said, "I need my nude heels to go with my dress. We have to stop by my place on the way, but I still have to do my makeup, pin up my hair, and get dressed. We're never going to make it in time."

He reached for his shirt. "You finish getting ready. I'll go get your heels."

Relief burst through her, and she threw her arms around him. "God I love you!" *Oh shit! Shitshitshit!* Twice in one day! She closed her eyes, telling herself to take it back, but she was *done* holding it in. If they could get past this one step, then telling him about the baby tonight would be easier. Drawing upon all of her courage, she said, "I *do*, Scotty. I love you." She stepped back, his uncomfortable gaze slicing her wide open, and the truth came out. "I love who you are and who I am with you, and I know you love me, too. I feel it when you touch me, and I see it when you look at me."

He didn't say a word. He just stood there, his jaw clenching, the torture in his eyes almost too much to bear.

"You can't even say it back to me?" Tears stung her eyes.

He stood rigid. "It's not that."

"Then what is it? They're *words*, Scott. Words you should want to say if you truly love me. I'm not asking for a ring, but if you can't even tell me you love me, then what are we doing?"

She didn't mean to raise her voice, but there was no holding back her pain.

"You know I love you, Penny, but those words come with a promise I can't make."

Tears slid down her cheeks. "The only promise they carry is one of love. I'm living out of a drawer and a bag, Scott, going back to my place every week to swap my clothes and bring more over. Do you know how that feels? Or what it's like to lie in your arms loving you so much it hurts to keep it in?"

"Of course I do," he said angrily. "I'm doing the same damn thing."

She grabbed his hands. "But don't you see? We don't have to hold back. What we have is so beautiful and so right, we should be celebrating it. I know you're scared of having kids because of all you went through, but you're not like your father. You're kind and loving, and you have the patience of a saint—"

"*Stop.*" He tore his hands away. "Do you have any idea who I see in the mirror every goddamn day? My *father*, Penny. A man who beat me and Sarah from the time we were little kids. You have no idea what it's like to see your sister beaten or cowering in the corner. Or to go after the man who was doing it, when you're too young and weak to stop him. One fucking punch from him sent me flying across the room, day after day, for *years*. And our goddamn mother calling Sarah heinous names all the time? Belittling us? I have no fucking idea how we survived, and I don't know if that type of monster is a part of *me*." He paced, gritting his teeth, nostrils flaring.

Tears blurred her vision.

"I love you with every fiber of my being, Penny. You're the fucking eye to every storm. You're my safe harbor. The world could be exploding around me, but when I look at you, when I hear your voice or feel your touch, nothing else matters. You make me feel whole and solid and so fucking good it's unreal." Tears glistened in his eyes. "I *want* what you want, to build a life free from duffel bags and wrong shoes. But I know how badly you want a family. I don't *think* I would ever hurt a kid, but I'm not willing to take that risk and bring children into this world when something inside me could snap and I could end up just like my fucking father." He turned away, hands curling into fists.

A crushing feeling in her chest emptied her lungs. She forced her legs to *move*, and she ran around him, putting her face in front of his, so he had to hear her. "But you're *not* him, Scotty. You love your nieces and nephews. Hell, you adore all the kids—Lulu, Kennedy, Lincoln. You're around kids all the time, and I've never heard you even yell at them."

He tried to turn away, but she moved with him and said, "Even though *I* know you'll never hurt a child, I understand why you are afraid, and I respect that. Please don't throw away something we both know is right when there are ways to deal with issues like these. We can go to therapy together, talk to a professional who can figure out if you have that type of anger inside of you. Therapy helped Roni and Quincy. I'm sure they can recommend someone. And I'll be by your side every step of the way. Whatever it takes, I'm there, all in."

He swallowed hard, and she thought he was going to say something. When he didn't, she said, "Look at your sisters. Sarah and Josie grew up in the same house as you, and they're loving parents. Why would you be any different?"

He gritted his teeth, shaking his head, slaying her anew. "Penny…" His eyes glistened with tears.

"*No*," she warned. "I'm not giving up on you, or on us, just because you're too afraid to rip off the bandage and see what's beneath it." She threw her arms around his body, holding him tight, praying he wouldn't end them, and was surprised that he embraced her back.

"I love you so fucking much it hurts me, too, Pen." He kissed the top of her head, holding her tighter. "But what if a therapist says I'm at risk? What then?" He took her by the arms, putting space between them, his anguished eyes driving a knife into her chest. "You'll have spent months, maybe years, falling deeper in love with me, and you'll never have the family you want. If that isn't a recipe for regret, I don't know what is."

Her heart shattered, sobs tearing from her lungs.

"This is my shit, sweetheart," he said in a gentler tone. His jaw tightened again, regret rising in his eyes. "You deserve a man who can give you everything you want."

Nonononono. "I want *you*," she said through sobs.

"I want you, too, because I'm a selfish prick. But that's not fair, because I might never be enough for you."

It took everything she had to force words through her swollen throat. "How can you know unless you try?"

He pulled her into his arms again, holding her even tighter than before, and said, "I don't," in a loving, sorrowful, broken voice.

Chapter Five

SCOTT STOOD AT a window in the five-story Davenport mansion, on the sought-after French-style country estate, gazing out at the impressive gardens where Bones and Sarah's wedding was going to take place. Stone planters overflowing with red flowers lined an aisle of red carpeting over a lush green lawn, anchored at the far end by a stone dome-topped gazebo, where they would say their vows. Just beyond the gazebo was a large reflecting pool and fountain, and on the other side of the pool was the elaborate stone colonnade where the reception would take place. Between their friends, family, Bones's professional colleagues, and members of the Dark Knights motorcycle club, of which Bones's father, Biggs, was the president, and Bones and his brothers Bullet and Bear were members, more than two hundred guests were milling about.

Scott's gaze moved over the crowd, quickly finding Penny, as if she were calling out to him. She was stunning with the sides of her hair pinned up and a few soft tendrils framing her face, wearing a peach off-the-shoulder dress with a breezy skirt and the nude heels they'd stopped to pick up on the way. They'd arrived a little late, but Sarah was as gracious as ever and hadn't said a word about it. He watched Penny playing with Hail, Kennedy, and Lincoln, and his gut knotted. He'd been envisioning her with *their* children for months. It was hard not to when they were around his sisters' kids so often. He imagined their little girls with big blue eyes, their honey hair twisted up with bows and ribbons, and lanky, shaggy-haired boys who loved the outdoors. They'd read them stories, teach them right from wrong, and shower them with so much love, all their kids' friends would say *they* were the lucky ones. He imagined teaching them to fish and sail and taking them to the library, ball games, and to Penny's shop to teach them how to make crazy ice cream sundaes with made-up names and too many toppings. He'd be their human jungle gym and their greatest protector, and Penny would look at him with the same stars in her eyes that she did when they babysat.

What a fucking fantasy that was.

He and Penny hadn't said more than a handful of words on the drive over, but their hands had remained tightly interlocked, as if they could save each other from his broken soul his parents had left behind.

Bones was giving Sarah the wedding of a lifetime, and Scott couldn't even promise Penny a fucking dresser.

"*Scott!*" Josie hollered, jarring him from his thoughts.

He shook his head and tried to focus on his petite youngest

sister, gorgeous in an above-the-knee pale-pink dress with a sweetheart neckline and a gauzy skirt, her strawberry-blonde hair falling in natural waves to her shoulders. Josie looked nothing like him and Sarah. She was pixieish, with an upturned nose, high cheekbones, a beauty mark just below the left corner of her mouth, and keen brown eyes, which were currently laden with worry. "Sorry, Josie."

"I called your name three times. What's going on with you? First you paced like a caged animal for ten minutes, and now you're off in la-la land."

"Are you okay?" Sarah asked, pushing to her feet from the chair in front of the makeup mirror.

Sarah was taller and curvier than Josie, with almond-shaped eyes and a straight nose. She was breathtaking in her wedding gown. The intricate lace bodice hugged her figure, and the skirt flared out like a ball gown with lace trailing down the length of the sides. Her long sandy hair was pinned up in an elegant twist with tiny white flowers weaved into it. She shared the same brown eyes as he and Josie, but even in the darkest of times, Sarah's had always been softer and kinder. The concern staring back at him brought a wave of guilt.

"Yeah, fine," he lied, walking away from the window. "You two look gorgeous. Bones and Jed are going to lose their minds."

Sarah and Josie exchanged worried glances.

"Okay, cut the crap," Josie said, crossing her arms. "Tell us what's wrong."

This was Sarah's special day, and he was determined not to burden them with his issues. He slipped a hand into his pocket as casually as he could and said, "It's just an emotional day. It's not every day your sister gets married."

Josie shook her head. "I'm not buying it. You were so frigging happy when I got married, you were all smiles and tears."

Scott feigned a smile. He'd done a fairly good job of hiding how overwhelmed he'd been that day, though Penny had seen right through his strong facade.

"Uh-oh." Sarah stepped closer and said, "Something's definitely wrong."

Scott gritted his teeth.

"Did you and Penny have a fight?" Josie asked.

"Oh no. Did you?" Sarah said empathetically.

He paced. "Can we not do this on your wedding day?"

"We're doing it." Josie fell into step beside him. "What happened?"

"Nothing."

"Nothing my butt," Josie snapped. "You never let me or Sarah do this to you. You make us spill our guts. So spill it."

Sarah stepped in front of him, blocking his path. "Now I'm going to worry all day if you don't tell us. Maybe we can help."

"Nobody can help," he said flatly.

"Have a little faith in us," Josie said.

"We had faith in you for all those years when we lived with Mom and Dad and you protected us," Sarah said sweetly.

"I never protected you well enough." The truth tasted ran-

.id.

He'd never forget the pain of being forced to leave them behind. He'd been planning their escape for years and had saved every cent he'd earned working at the marina throughout high school. One of the older guys he worked with had hooked him up with a fake ID and opened a bank account where Scott had stashed his savings. But a few weeks before the date he'd hoped to leave with the girls, he'd come home from work and his father had given him hell for something. He couldn't even remember now what it was. Scott had been fighting back forever, but he'd recently hit a growth spurt and stood eye-to-eye with his father. When his father got in his face and pushed him against the wall, Scott went after him with everything he had. He'd been blinded by rage, punching and shouting, and his father had given it right back to him. Fists and blood were flying. Josie had been only thirteen and Sarah sixteen, both of them screaming and crying. Josie was huddled in a corner, Sarah stood in front of her, protecting her as their mother shouted at them to shut up. Sweet, delicate Sarah had jumped on their father's back, trying to pull him off Scott, and their mother had gone after her, slapping her on her face and back and clawing at her, and Scott had lost it. He slugged his father so hard he'd cracked open his knuckles, and then he'd shoved his mother away from the girls, hollering for Sarah to get Josie downstairs. Thank God she'd listened so they didn't have to witness the worst of it. He'd gotten his father in a choke hold, and then he'd thrown him across the room, intending to get the girls and leave. But his father had threatened to have him arrested for assault and kidnapping. At seventeen, with no reported history of abuse, it would have been his word against his father's, and the charges probably would have stuck. Scott couldn't take the risk of being hauled into jail and the girls going right back to those monsters. He'd given Sarah the bank card, told her to guard it with her life, and that he'd get another job and put more money in the account. He left, intending to come back for them in a day or two, but his fucking father had reported him to the police after all, and they were looking for him. In desperation, he'd stolen two hundred bucks from a convenience store, bringing his savings to four hundred for the girls. His friend helped him hide out in another town until things calmed down, but by the time he went back, his sisters were gone without a trace.

"Yes you did, Scott," Sarah insisted. "If you hadn't been there for us for all those years, I might not be alive today."

"What is this really about, Scott?" Josie asked. "What does that have to do with Penny? You guys were all over each other last night."

"Nothing. *Everything*," he admitted. "I'm fucked up, terrified that I've got that bastard in me."

Josie shook her head. "That's crazy. You're amazing with the kids."

"It's not crazy," Sarah said solemnly.

Scott's stomach plummeted.

"I was terrified that I'd be like them, too," Sarah admitted.

I kept waiting for the monster in me to come out. When I had Bradley and Lila, I stayed up at night, afraid if I slept, I'd wake up a different person. I think that's normal after what we've been through. Josie, you never had to live on the streets, with an abuser, or on an oil rig with no one to show you any love. *Thank God* you had Brian, and he loved and cherished you from the moment you left home with him. You were so young, I think he washed away most of your fears. But our experiences were different and left brutal scars."

"What about when you had Maggie Rose, Sarah? Did you worry then?" Scott asked.

"No. I already had two babies, and I wasn't fearing for my life anymore. I had Bones, and I had you and Josie and the Whiskeys and all of our friends. I understand your fears, Scott. We lived every minute not knowing if it would be our last, and you endured it longer than any of us." Sarah took his hand, looking at him with empathy, not pity, and said, "But do you remember when we got into the accident? You had a collapsed lung and two broken legs, and you fought to help us get out of the car. As soon as you saw Bullet reaching for us, you told him to get the babies and me, over and over. Even after he had us all out, I still heard you saying it." Her eyes dampened. "And when you woke up after surgery, the nurses had to hold you down because you were out of your mind with worry over us. You wanted to get to us *that* badly, and you'd only known my kids a few weeks."

Scott remembered the fear that had gripped him that night.

He'd thought he'd lost them all after having only just found Sarah again.

"You're more patient with our kids than Sarah and I are. You never even lose your temper with them," Josie said.

"And not only that," Sarah said. "You took me and Josie and our children into your home and treated our kids like your own. You bathed them, changed diapers, fed them, took them out places, put them to sleep. You helped teach them what it means to be a family and how to love like a family should. It's been more than a decade since we got out of that house. If you were capable of what our parents did to us, we'd have seen signs of it by now. You're not a monster, Scott. You're just scared, and that's okay."

The door flew open, and Red Whiskey breezed in. "Who's ready to get—" Her smile faded, and her eyes narrowed, making her look even more like her doppelgänger, Sharon Osbourne. "Oh boy. What's going on in here? Please tell me it's not cold feet, because my son is going to jump out of his skin if I don't get you down that aisle soon."

"Don't worry, Red. My feet are hot to trot. Nothing could stop me from saying I do to my wonderful Bones," Sarah said with a grin.

"*Whew*," Red said.

"I'm just working on my shit, Red," Scott admitted to the woman who had welcomed him and his sisters and all their children into her family with open arms.

"Ah," Red said, as if she'd heard it a million times. "Your

heart is kicking you in the ass, isn't it?"

"Something like that," Scott said.

Red's expression softened. "That's a good thing, honey. It's the men who don't realize they have shit to work on that we worry about." She turned to the girls and said, "Dixie has made Bradley and Lila practice their walks down the aisle so many times, they're going to do it in their sleep. Let's go, ladies. We have a wedding to get to!"

"Yes!" Sarah exclaimed as they followed Red and Josie down the hall.

Scott took Sarah's hand and said, "Remember how nervous you were when you went on your first date with Bones? And look at you now. I'm so happy for you. You and Josie deserve all the happiness in the world."

"So do you, Scott," Sarah said as they descended the steps and headed for the back door.

"Thanks. I'm sorry for raining on your parade."

"Don't be silly. Just don't rain on your own parade." She leaned closer to him as they crossed the marble floor and said, "Our parents are dead and gone. They can no longer hurt us. Don't let their evilness overshadow your greatness. Penny loves you, Scott, and I *know* you love her. Let that love shine through, and the rest will come naturally."

If only love were enough…

Penny wanted, and *deserved*, far more than just his love.

TODAY WAS SUPPOSED to be perfect. Penny had envisioned a morning full of love, laughter, holding hands, and swoon-worthy compliments about how devastatingly handsome Scott looked in his tuxedo, which would be met with the same enthusiastic flattery about how great she looked in her new dress, followed by lustful kisses and endless temptation, leaving them longing to be in each other's arms at the end of the day. Instead she was stuck sitting between Finlay and Quincy, holding back a river of tears caused by heartfelt confessions and insurmountable confusion, followed by a few forced words on the drive to the wedding. If that wasn't enough torture for one day, Finlay was snuggling too-cute-for-words Tallulah in her frilly pink dress and matching booties and ogling her burly husband, who was standing with Bear by the stone gazebo where Bones and Sarah would say their vows, and Quincy was smooching with Roni. In the row in front of them were several of Penny's other friends. Truman and Gemma were loving up Kennedy and Lincoln, and Jed and Hail were playing a game on Jed's phone and laughing up a storm. Bear's wife, Crystal, was cuddling her adorable eight-month-old, and Dixie's husband, Jace, was tickling the baby's belly. Jace had been all over Dixie, trying to get her to agree to start their family.

Penny was *literally* surrounded by people in love.

Her gaze drifted to her single girlfriends, Tracey and Izzy,

61

.ing farther down that row. *Maybe I should have sat there.*

That thought brought a rush of hot tears. She squeezed her eyes shut to keep them from falling. She didn't want to be single.

"*Hey,* Pen." Quincy nudged her arm.

She opened her eyes and closed her mouth tightly, willing the tears not to fall. But her sadness was too great. Her lower lip still trembled, and a lone, traitorous tear escaped down her cheek.

Quincy reached into the pocket of his suitcoat and handed her a wad of tissues. "I came prepared. Remember how much Roni bawled at Josie and Jed's wedding?"

"Thank you." She wiped her eyes, but thinking about Josie and Jed, another couple who'd fallen so hard for each other Jed had put a ring on Josie's finger to make sure the world knew it, had her struggling to hold back more tears. Penny pressed the wad of tissues to her eyes.

"You okay?" Finlay asked.

The worry in Finlay's voice only made her cry harder.

Quincy leaned closer. "Penny, what's going on?"

"Nothing," she choked out, wiping her eyes.

"You lie about as well as I would if I tried," Quincy said. "Want to take a walk? Talk about it?"

That made her heart hurt even more. She didn't want to lay her heart on the line with Quincy and bring him down. She wanted the impossible—to go back in time and change Scott's response. To hear him say he loved her too much to let her go, and he wanted a family. Tears poured down her cheeks.

Roni peered around Quincy and said, "Oh gosh, Penny. What's wrong?"

Penny shot to her feet. "I just need a minute. I'm going to the ladies' room."

"I'll go with you," Finlay said, reaching for Tallulah's baby bag.

"Me too," Roni said as she and Finlay stood.

Their friends in the next row turned around in their seats, and Gemma said, "Where are you guys going? The wedding is about to start."

The music began, and all the guests turned around in their seats to see Bones's parents, Red and Biggs, walking out of the mansion toward the aisle. Penny's stomach plummeted. She was trapped.

As she and the other girls took their seats, Quincy whispered, "Want to talk?"

Penny shook her head.

"Here if you need me," he whispered, giving her arm a reassuring squeeze.

If she told Quincy she needed to get out of there, he'd plow down the aisle and make it happen. *So would Scott. But if he saw me this upset, he'd probably pick me up and carry me.*

A lump lodged in her throat. At least now that the wedding was starting, she had a reasonable excuse for her tears. Everyone knew she cried at weddings.

"Tell me what's going on," Finlay whispered.

"Nothing."

Finlay made a puckered-lips, squinty-eyed face that Penny knew her big sister believed to be a scowl. Penny had never had the heart to tell Finlay that she sucked at scowling and that face made her look like a blond fairy getting ready to accept a kiss she didn't want.

Luckily, the procession started, and Finlay turned to watch her in-laws walk down the aisle, giving Penny a moment to try to compose herself. She breathed deeply, thinking about Scott. On the drive over, they'd agreed not to let their issues ruin Sarah's wedding. When they'd arrived, Dixie had rushed over to take Scott up to Sarah. Before going with her, he'd pulled Penny into his arms, holding her tighter than ever before, and said, *Promise me a dance.* She'd promised, and as he'd walked away, she'd felt like she'd promised a *last* dance, and her heart had shattered all over again.

The lump in her throat expanded painfully, and she tried to focus on Red and Biggs as they made their way down the aisle. Red was gorgeous in a floor-length rose-colored gown with short lace sleeves that set off her fiery red hair, and Biggs couldn't look more handsome in a black tuxedo and bow tie, which was partially covered by his long, graying beard. He'd suffered a stroke years ago and walked with a cane. Penny's thoughts pedaled back to Scott's recovery after the car accident, when he'd needed to use a cane. She couldn't remember a single time when he'd complained about his injuries or the pain from them. Once she'd learned the extent of his childhood abuse, she'd had the heart-wrenching thought that the injuries from his accident were probably less painful than the abuse he'd suffered, as they weren't caused by someone who should have loved him.

Penny caught movement out of the corner of her eye and realized she'd been staring off into space. She really needed to turn off her brain, because tears were streaming down her cheeks again. Swiping at them with the tissues, she focused on the procession. Dixie, Bradley, and Maggie Rose were just starting to walk down the aisle. Dixie, a tall, slender redhead, looked elegant in a short pale-pink dress with a crisscross bodice and a flowy knee-length skirt. Bradley was too cute for words in his tuxedo and bow tie, holding the handle of the white Cinderella wedding carriage with a lace canopy that Bear had built for him to pull Maggie Rose down the aisle. The carriage had large white wheels, pink roses decorating the sides, and fluffy pink and white tulle surrounded the white silk pillows that cushioned Maggie Rose. She was adorable in a white frilly dress with a floral headband.

"No running, Aunt Dixie," Bradley announced.

Chuckles rose from the guests, and Bradley grinned proudly as he pulled his sister down the aisle, waving and calling out to everyone he knew, "Hi, Aunt Finlay! Hi, Lulu! Hi, Penny..." earning more laughter. Behind them, Lila held Josie's hand as they walked down the aisle. Lila looked like a princess in a white dress with a fluffy skirt and a pink bow in her wispy blond hair. Josie was gorgeous in her pale-pink dress, her loving eyes zeroing in on Jed and Hail, bringing Penny more tears.

When they reached the end of the aisle, Red scooped up Maggie Rose, and she and Biggs took the children to sit in the front row, while Dixie and Josie took their places across from the Whiskey men by the gazebo.

There was a brief moment of silence before "A Thousand Years" by Christina Perri began playing, and Scott and Sarah walked out of the mansion. Penny's heart lurched. Sarah was stunning in her wedding gown, but Penny's eyes were riveted to the man standing proudly by her side, the man Penny felt like she'd loved for a thousand years and *wanted* to love for a trillion more. Tears poured down her cheeks as Scott's gaze found hers. His brows knitted, love and sadness coalescing in his beautiful eyes, drawing a sob from Penny's chest. She covered her mouth, and Scott watched her until they'd passed her row. She wanted him with all her heart. She wanted everything with him—their baby, saying *I do* in front of all their friends, a future of pancakes and boat rides. She wanted to give Scott all the love he'd missed out on and so much more that he'd feel it even if they were on opposite sides of the world.

Quincy touched her arm and whispered, "Now, *that's* the look of love."

She knew he was talking about the way Bones was looking at Sarah as she took her place across from him, but Penny was still drawn to Scott, now standing beside Josie but looking at *her*. Her heart ached for the love billowing between them.

Scott may not think he would be a good daddy, but she knew in her heart he'd be one of the best. Nevertheless, her love for him was speaking louder than anything else. As they took their seats, she was glad she hadn't told him about the baby yet. Scott was an honorable man who would do the right thing by her and their child. But Penny didn't want him to do the *honorable* thing. She didn't want a husband and a father for her child who felt trapped. She'd made a mistake that morning, selfishly trying to get him to see himself as she saw him and to change his mind.

She placed her hand protectively over her belly, making the hardest decision of her life.

She could find her way as a single mother, even if losing Scott would mean never feeling whole again, but she could never forgive herself if Scott felt trapped into a role that terrified him.

As sobs fell from her lips and Finlay squeezed her hand, Penny knew what she had to do. She just hoped she would survive it.

Chapter Six

THE CEREMONY WAS beautiful and just long enough to leave everyone teary-eyed. Sarah cried as she and Bones said their vows, the love in their voices so thick it was palpable. Every time Penny's and Scott's eyes had connected, it deepened the ache in her chest, making her cry harder. She'd given up even trying to stop the rivers of tears that plagued her.

After the ceremony, Hawk Pennington, the photographer and a Dark Knight, had swept the wedding party and their spouses away for pictures in the gardens. Cocktail hour was in full swing in the stone colonnade. Music from the DJ filled the air as people mingled, enjoying appetizers and cocktails and dancing. Fancy tables with elaborate floral centerpieces surrounded the dance floor, and gorgeous iron and stone planters around the perimeter of the colonnade boasted pink and white roses. The stone columns were wrapped with strings of white lights, and more strands of lights were draped overhead. It was absolutely magical.

Penny stood with her friends, listening to them talk about the wedding, while she sneaked glances at Scott who was posing for pictures with his family. Everyone in the wedding party was paired off except him. She longed to be by his side. Even from that distance, she could tell by his body language that his smiles were forced. Guilt pressed in on her for clouding what should have been one of the happiest days of his life.

"Speaking of grand gestures," Gemma said, pulling Penny from her thoughts. Gemma was gorgeous in a forest-green dress that hugged her petite frame; her brown hair was pinned up in a fancy twist. "Roni just told us that you got into the dessert festival next year. Why didn't you say something last night? That's so exciting!"

"I was bursting at the seams to tell everyone, but it was Bones and Sarah's big night, and I didn't want to steal their thunder." That wasn't completely true. Of course Penny was excited to share her news about the amazing things Scott had done for her, but the pregnancy had distracted her from everything else. The only thing she'd been bursting to say last night was *I love you* to Scott and *We're going to have a baby.*

Thank goodness when her seams had finally burst, she'd held *that* news back.

"I gave Scott a copy of the article I wrote about Luscious Licks a few years ago for the community newspaper, and Tru and I gave you a rave review." Gemma glanced briefly at Kennedy and Lincoln twirling around Truman on the dance floor. "We told Alyssa all about the special sundaes you make on

...ne spot for the kids and how you always take time to talk with them. I hope it helped."

"And Dixie and I went through her pictures and gathered shots of your ice cream stands at a few of the fundraisers," Tracey said. She looked gorgeous in a short blue halter dress, a sexy choice for a girl who was far more demure than her snarky roommate and coworker at Whiskey Bro's, Izzy, who was flaunting her hot body in a tight yellow dress that showed off her curves.

"Wait a second. You guys knew about what Scott did?" Penny couldn't believe Scott had reached out to everyone. "I never saw any of the reviews or the pictures he sent or anything. The whole thing was a surprise. Thank you for helping him and saying nice things about me."

"We all knew about it, Pen. Everyone contributed, and you deserved every compliment and more," Quincy said, looking handsome in his dark suit, with his hair slicked back and an arm around Roni, beautiful in a floral dress, her brown hair flowing over her shoulders. "You should know Scott pursued that woman relentlessly for you. He's crazy about you, Pen."

Quincy held her gaze, and she knew he was letting his words sink in. He had pulled her aside right after the ceremony to try again to get her to open up to him. She didn't want to end up in tears again, but she also hadn't wanted to lie, so she'd told him that she and Scott had gotten into a tiff that morning. She knew he didn't buy it, because she and Scott had never fought before. They talked things out. Well, everything except the most important subjects: love, marriage, and babies, which they kept pushing to the periphery of their relationship. Luckily, Quincy knew her well enough to realize she didn't want to talk about it, and he'd said, *My shoulder is your shoulder when and if you need it.* When he'd hugged her, she'd had to stifle more tears.

She'd finally dammed the rivers and hoped she could keep her tears at bay for the rest of the reception.

"I know he is," she said as Scott's words came back to her. *I love you with every fiber of my being, Penny. You're the fucking eye to every storm, my safe harbor. The world could be exploding around me, but when I look at you, when I hear your voice or feel your touch, nothing else matters.* Except other things did matter, like the life they'd created inside her.

"I've got to hand it to Scott. He's one clever fox. I bet *my* review nailed it for you. I wrote about the sundaes you *don't* advertise." Izzy waggled her dark brows. "Like the Triple O and the Heavenly Hookup."

"With reviews like that, it's a wonder Alyssa Braden didn't hightail it over to Peaceful Harbor to check out the single guys," Tracey said.

Everyone laughed, including Penny, and boy, did she need that laugh.

Izzy nudged Tracey and said, "Speaking of single men, Mr. Hard Body is looking pretty delicious in that suit."

Penny followed Izzy's gaze to Desmond "Diesel" Black striding across the dance floor, stoic faced, eyes trained on Tracey. Diesel was a bartender at Whiskey Bro's and a Nomad

Dark Knight. His crisp white shirt strained across his bulbous biceps and chest, his slacks stretched to the limit over his massive thighs. Talk about a man of few words, Diesel grunted more than he spoke, and Penny swore he looked like he was going to throw Tracey over his shoulder and haul her off to his cave.

"Wow. He sure cleans up nicely." Roni gazed lovingly at Quincy and said, "But not quite as nice as my guy."

Tracey was staring at Diesel like it was the first time she'd ever seen him.

"Did you ever find out why he wanted to know if you had a date for the wedding?" Gemma asked.

Tracey scoffed, though her eyes never left Diesel as she said, "When I learn how to decipher a grunt, I'll let you know what the reason was."

"Uncle Diesel!" Kennedy skipped over to Diesel in her frilly blue dress and Mary Janes, stopping him by the edge of the dance floor. His chiseled features didn't soften as Kennedy took his hand and pulled him toward the middle of the floor.

A few feet away, Lincoln was standing on Truman's feet, holding his hands as they danced. Penny warmed at the sight of them, picturing Scott doing the same with their baby one day. The lump that had lodged in her throat earlier returned with a vengeance. Why did she even play with those thoughts?

As her friends talked, Penny gazed out at the gardens and saw Scott making a beeline for her. His jaw was tight, chin low, making her stomach twist into knots.

Roni moved closer to her and said, "Now, that's a man on a mission if I've ever seen one."

Penny got more nervous with Scott's every step as he closed the distance between them. She told herself not to make a scene, to hold herself together, but she felt nauseous, and she didn't know if it was the pregnancy or the fact that since she'd decided to do the only fair thing, she was afraid if she opened her mouth, it would tumble out.

Panic rose in Penny's chest, and she turned away from Scott to try to regain control just as Lincoln ran off the dance floor, hollering, *"DancewifmeBooful!"* He grabbed Roni's hand, tugging her toward the dance floor.

Penny focused on a spot on the floor in an effort to calm herself down.

"Little dude, you're always stealing my girl," Quincy joked. "Hey, Pen…?" He touched her arm. "You don't look so good. Are you okay?"

She knew what she had to do. Drawing upon all of her courage, Penny said, "No, but hopefully I will be." As Scott stepped into the colonnade, she looked at Quincy and said, "Save me a spot on your shoulder, will you?"

THERE WAS A storm brewing inside Scott, and if he didn't stop it, it was going to drown him. It had been torture watching

Penny cry during the ceremony knowing it was his fault. He'd wanted to take her into his arms and apologize for the hell he'd caused. On top of that, standing for family photographs without her had left him feeling off-balance and empty. He couldn't take it anymore.

"Hey, sweets," he said gruffly. "Can you come with me, please?"

He reached for her hand, and as she took it, the smile that usually lit up the room barely reached her eyes, cutting him like a knife. She went with him, but he felt a difference in her touch and in the energy she gave off, as if she'd already erected a wall between them.

"Where are we going?" she asked in a pained voice as they made their way across the lawn.

"I want you in the pictures with us."

"*What?*" Penny stopped cold, tears welling in her eyes. "No." She took a step back, shaking her head. "I can't be in the pictures with you and your family when I don't know if we're even going to be together tomorrow." Her voice escalated as tears streamed down her cheeks. "I can't...I can't do this."

"I can't either, Pen. I—"

"Don't!" she shouted, sobs distorting the word. "Don't say it." She turned and stalked away from him and the reception.

He went after her, gently taking her hand, and said, "Please, just hear me out."

"I can't do this *here*," she hissed. "I don't want everyone witnessing you breaking up with me. I know you don't want kids, and you know I do, and I love you too much to force you into a life you don't want." Sobs tumbled out, and she covered her face with her hands, talking from behind them. "God! Just say it. Get it over with."

"Sweetheart, I am so sorry for making you cry." He gathered her quaking body in his arms, his heart swelling and breaking at once. "I don't want to end things with you, Penny. I can't imagine a day without you, much less a lifetime."

She seemed to hold her breath, her face still buried in his chest. Then she tipped her face up, eyes swollen and confused, nose pink, and cheeks as wet as rain. "*What?*"

He cradled her face in his hands, wiping her tears with his thumbs. His heart was beating so hard, he was sure she could feel it pounding between them. "I'm so scared of becoming my father, I almost let it ruin the best thing I've ever had. But I'm not going to let that bastard take one more thing from me. I love you so damn much, Penny. I never wanted—*want*—to hurt or disappoint you, and I realized today that you and my sisters are right. I *love* children. I love their smiles, their laughter, their cuddles. I love them too much to ever hurt them. But the fear is *real*, Penny, and I can't just shake it off. When I was standing down there with all the guys and their wives and children, I realized that I didn't have to shake it off. Being scared is the *solution*, not the *problem*."

"I don't understand." She blinked repeatedly. "What are you saying? What solution?"

"I'm saying that instead of giving in to the fear and letting it in us, I'll go to therapy, figure out where that fear is buried, and dig that son of a bitch out. I'll take that fear apart piece by piece until I have all my shit figured out."

Hope rose in her eyes, bringing more tears. "You will?"

"*Yes.* I love you, Penny. You're my soul mate, my best friend, my eye of the fucking storm, and I want our clothes in *one* closet and a dresser just for you. I want little girls who wrap me around their tiny fingers, keep their hair up with colorful clips and straws, and dole out love like they have an endless supply. I want little boys who run through the woods, jump off docks, and protect their sisters from snakes and bullies—but never have to worry about protecting them from me."

Her tears flooded against his thumbs, and a sob fell from her lips.

"I'm *all in*, sweetheart. In for a penny, in for a pound, and I will stop at *nothing* to become the man that you deserve."

"Oh, *Scotty!*" She threw her arms around him, sobbing against his chest. "You've *always* been the man that I deserve."

She clung to him like she wanted to burrow deep inside him. But she was already there, as much a part of him as the air he breathed, easing the storm.

"Do you think you can handle *six* or *seven* pounds?" she asked as she took his hand, but he didn't understand the question. She placed his hand on her belly, a gorgeous smile lighting up the hope in her eyes.

Understanding came with a jolt of shock. "*You're…We're…?*" Joy and fear intertwined, stealing his ability to speak.

"Yes. I took three tests."

Three tests. "We're having a baby?"

She nodded. She was having a baby. His baby. *Their* baby.

Our baby.

You're having our baby.

Holy shit we're having a baby.

Images of little Pennys with radiant smiles and loving hearts flashed in his mind, and like kryptonite to Superman, happiness obliterated his fear, and "We're having a *baby*!" came rushing out. Penny laughed as he lifted her off her feet and crushed his lips to hers.

"God, I love you," he said between kisses. "A *baby*. We're having a baby!"

He couldn't believe how elated he was or how *free* he felt. He kissed her again, longer this time, and as the rest of the world came back into focus, cheers and claps broke through his haze of stunned elation, and he realized they were surrounded by their families and friends, who were cheering and clapping. His sisters were crying, along with half the women there, and Hawk was taking pictures. He looked around them as he set Penny on her feet, keeping her tucked against him.

Kennedy barreled toward them, yelling, "I wanna name your baby!"

He and Penny laughed, and he gazed into her gorgeous glittering eyes and said, "How do you feel about a five-year-old naming our baby?"

"How bad can it be? She named Tallulah."

"I like Moana!" Kennedy said.

Everyone laughed.

"Want to rethink your answer?" Scott asked.

Penny wrapped both arms around him and said, "As long as I get you and our baby, that's all that matters."

"*Babies*, sweetheart." He kissed her again and said, "We have too much love in our hearts to hoard it."

MUCH LATER, AFTER apologizing to Sarah and Bones for intruding on their big day, being passed from one congratulatory embrace to the next, and posing for loads of pictures, which Sarah and Bones insisted Hawk take to commemorate what had also become Penny and Scott's special day, Penny was still on cloud nine. Toasts were made, Sarah and Bones danced their first dance to "It's You" by Maggie Rose, the artist they named their daughter for, and after a delicious meal, Scott led Penny out to the dance floor.

When he took her in his arms and gazed lovingly into her eyes, she noticed the shadows were gone. He seemed lighter, happier. She felt it in his embrace, too. Gone was the underlying tether she'd once felt, as if taking charge of his fears had cut it loose.

"Do you remember our first real date?" he asked.

"How could I ever forget? That was the day you let me into your heart."

It was a cold Sunday in early November, and they'd taken his boat to Capshaw Island, a small fishing town with wild ponies, a wildlife sanctuary, and not much commercialization. They'd walked through the town and gone out to the beach where the ponies ran free. They'd cuddled up, bundled in blankets, and watched the ponies for the longest time. She'd never forget the way he'd slowly relaxed, letting go of the tension she hadn't even realized he'd carried until that very moment on the beach. The same tension, she now understood, he'd possessed every day since, until just hours ago. That day on the island was the first time he'd told her about the abuse he and Sarah had suffered, the fear he and his siblings had lived with, and the guilt he'd felt for not being able to protect Sarah from their parents' wrath or Josie from the fights she'd been forced to watch.

He touched his lips to hers as they danced and said, "I realize now that I never finished letting you in. I've been living inside a suit of armor, trying to protect everyone else in case my father was inside of me. But when I realized I was going to lose you, I knew I had to find a way to break free from it and see what was left. It turns out it wasn't my father inside after all. It was fear of becoming him eating me alive. I'd trapped it inside myself for so long, I had no idea how else to be. You changed that, sweetheart. Your love set me free. I am going to do all the things I promised, and I'm sure it won't be easy for either of us.

hank you for seeing in me what I never allowed myself to see. I'm sorry it took me so long to get to this point."

She hadn't thought it was possible to love him more than she already did, but now she knew she was wrong. "I would have waited forever for you, Scotty, even if it meant living in separate houses and raising our child together but apart. I knew in my heart that one day you'd see yourself as I always have and come back to us. That day just came a lot sooner than I thought possible, and I am so glad it did."

He touched his forehead to hers and said, "I love you, sweets." He stopped dancing and lowered himself down in front of her, placing his hands to her belly, and said, "I'm going to be the best damn daddy this world has ever seen."

He pressed a kiss to her belly, and tears sprang to Penny's eyes. In that moment, beneath the twinkling lights of the colonnade, surrounded by the people they loved most, with a lifetime of love ahead of them, she knew that together they could handle the highs, the lows, and everything in between.

Chapter Seven

THE SMELL OF melted butter wafted into the living room, making Penny's mouth water as she queued up *The Proposal* on their television. At fourteen weeks pregnant, she had so many cravings, no food group was safe—including *boyfriend à la mode*.

It had been two months since Bones and Sarah's wedding, seven weeks since Penny had moved in with Scott, and two weeks since they'd heard the baby's heartbeat. She placed her hand over her tiny belly, remembering how she and Scott had cried when they'd heard it. She hadn't expected him to cry, too, but he'd been surprising her a lot lately. Not a day went by when he didn't kiss her belly or talk to the baby. He'd even begun asking about paint colors for the second bedroom to make it into a nursery.

"Are you making popcorn?" she called out to him in the kitchen where he was getting her a dish of ice cream.

"Yeah. You want some with your ice cream?"

She turned to look at him, shirtless on the other side of the half wall. She swore he looked even more handsome every day.

"Yes, please," Penny said. "Would you mind bringing a bowl of blueberries, too?"

He laughed. "You've got it, sweets." His gaze traveled down her body. She was still wearing the off-the-shoulder pink blouse and black miniskirt she'd worn to Roni's solo dance performance earlier that evening, which was incredible. "*Mm-mm.* I am one lucky man. You are stunning."

"You're not so bad yourself." She blew him a kiss.

"I thought up a new sundae for you."

He was always coming up with new ideas for her shop. His latest was the *We're* Having a Baby sundae, a banana split made to look like a baby carriage with Oreos as wheels.

"Yay! I'm going to have to buy a bigger chalkboard for the shop at this rate. What is it?"

"I'm making it for you. I'll show you when I bring it out."

She could hardly believe how wholly he was embracing fatherhood, but he'd changed in other ways, too. He was more open, talking about the future like he never would have before. Their lovemaking had changed, too. Sometimes Scott was even more loving and tender, *and* other times he was animalistic, a little rough and exploratory—and she loved both. She knew those changes had to do with how much trust he'd gained in himself and how much closer they'd become since he'd started therapy the week after she'd moved in.

He'd gone to his first session alone and had asked her to

join him from then on. It wasn't easy for either of them, even though Quincy and Roni, who had both gone through therapy, had warned them about the ways in which it could dredge up repressed feelings and memories. Penny hadn't been prepared for how much it hurt to see Scott reliving those awful times. But she was glad he allowed her to be by his side as they learned to navigate his past to clear a way to their future. It had given her more insight and understanding about why he'd worn that armor he'd described the day of the wedding and why it had been so difficult to strip it away.

She'd always known Scott was brave, but therapy had taken another type of courage and strength, proving once again that there was nothing Scott Beckley couldn't accomplish.

"Is that another cravings smile?" Scott asked.

She hadn't realized she was staring. "Yes, but not for food." Feeling extra frisky, she said, "Actually, you should bring the whipped cream with you."

His eyes heated, sending images of him lying naked on the couch with whipped cream on his...

Stopstopstop!

She couldn't get enough of him lately. When she'd told Finlay that her hormones had gone wild, her sister had said, *Just wait until you hit your fourth and fifth month. You'll want to tie him to the bed twenty-four hours a day.*

Penny was already there.

He came out of the kitchen carrying a massive bowl piled high with ice cream, hot fudge, whipped cream, blueberries, chocolate chips, cherries, and rainbow sprinkles.

"Holy cow, Scotty!" She sat up to get a better look as he placed the bowl on the coffee table. "Did you use the whole half gallon?"

"Every drop."

"I hope we're sharing it," she said, looking over the enormous sundae. "This looks delicious. What do you call it?"

"I call it the Will You Marry Me sundae." He dropped to one knee and turned the sundae around, revealing an ice cream altar with a plastic bride and groom holding hands beside a tiny baby carriage.

Penny's jaw dropped in disbelief, her eyes filling with tears. "*Ohmygod.*"

He took her hand, the brightest smile she'd ever seen curving his lips as he said, "I've practiced this a hundred times over the last month, and I knew exactly what I was going to say. But now my heart is racing, and you're so beautiful, and you're *here* in *our* house, on *our* couch, building a life with me that I never imagined having, and I can barely think straight." Tears glistened in his eyes, drawing more from her, as he said, "I want *more*, Penny. I want the world to know you're mine and I'm yours. I want our babies to grow up with parents they can count on to stick it out through thick and thin, and after what we've gone through these last couple of months, I know there's nothing we can't handle. I want to make love on our boat, take our kids to all the places we've explored together, and I want to find your hair clips in our couch when we're old and gray."

Nervous laughter bubbled out.

"You gave me the courage to let myself love wholly and freely and to be the man I'm supposed to be. You stuck by my side, and I want to stick by yours forever. Penelope Anne Wilson, will you marry me?"

"Yes!" She threw her arms around his neck, kissing him hard, her salty tears slipping between their lips. "I love you so much, Scotty. I can't *wait* to be your wife."

"And I can't wait to be your husband."

He reached behind the sundae and held up a small black box with a pink bow on it, which he must have hidden there when he set it down. "I know your father used to celebrate your milestones with gifts with pink bows on them. I hope this is okay."

"It's more than okay," she said shakily.

He opened the box and held up a ring. She'd never seen anything so beautiful and elegant. A halo of white diamonds circled a halo of chocolate diamonds, and in the center was a stunning canary diamond, all shimmering under the lights.

"*Scotty*," she said shakily. "I've never seen anything like it."

"It's one of a kind, like you." As he put it on her finger, he said, "A woman who makes sundaes that bring sunshine into everyone else's life deserves something just as magical in her own."

"I have something magical in my life. I have *you*."

"And Moana," he said, making them both laugh.

"You've given me everything I could ever want—a reason to

smile every morning when I wake up in your loving arms, a home to call our own, and our happy little family in the making."

"And we're going to have a hell of a lot of fun making it." He lowered his lips to hers, sealing their promises, and their futures, with their best kisses yet—kisses of a husband and wife to be.

Ready for More Whiskeys?

Fall in love with Tracey and Diesel in RUNNING ON DIESEL

Desmond "Diesel" Black is a Nomad with the Dark Knights motorcycle club. He protects others with his life and always rides alone. Tracey Kline left the only family she had for a man who broke more than her spirit, leaving her untrusting and on her own. When a twist of fate reveals pieces of the other no one else sees, will they be able to help each other mend their past hurts and learn to trust the chemistry and connection that's too strong to deny?

Meet the Colorado Whiskeys at Redemption Ranch

and fall in love with the Bradens in SEARCHING FOR LOVE

Zev Braden and Carly Dylan were childhood best friends, co-explorers, and first loves. Their close-knit families were sure they were destined to marry—until a devastating tragedy broke the two lovers apart. Over the next decade Zev, a nomadic treasure hunter, rarely returned to his hometown, and Carly became a chocolatier, building a whole new life across the country. When a chance encounter brings them back into each other's lives, can they find the true love that once existed, or will shattered dreams and broken hearts prevail? Find out in *Searching for Love*, a deliciously sexy, funny, and emotional second-chance romance.

Ready for More Dark Knights?

Meet the Dark Knights at Bayside and fall in love with the Wickeds, cousins to our beloved Whiskeys!

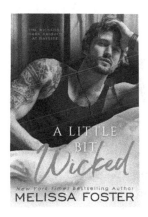

What do a cocky biker and a businesswoman who has sworn off dating bad boys have in common? According to Chloe Mallery, not much. But she couldn't be more wrong…

Justin came into the Wicked family after a harsh upbringing by a thieving father. He's gone through a lot to become a true Wicked, and he's made them proud. Now he's ready to show the woman he loves exactly what type of man he is. But Chloe has worked hard to move past her difficult upbringing, and she's wary of getting involved with a man who looks like he's walked right out of it. When tragedy strikes, will their trying pasts draw them together, or will Justin's protective nature be too much for Chloe's independent heart to accept?

Remember to download your Whiskey/Wicked family tree here:
www.MelissaFoster.com/Wicked-Whiskey-Family-Tree

Love Melissa's Writing?

If this is your first introduction to Melissa's work, please note that the Whiskeys are just one of the many family series in Melissa's Love in Bloom big-family romance collection. All Love in Bloom romances can be enjoyed as stand-alone novels. Characters appear in other family series, so you never miss out on an engagement, wedding, or birth. Discover more Love in Bloom magic and the collection here:
www.MelissaFoster.com/love-bloom-series

Melissa offers several free first-in-series ebooks. You can find them here:
www.MelissaFoster.com/LIBFree

Downloadable series checklists, reading orders, and more can be found on Melissa's Reader Goodies page.

More Books By Melissa Foster

LOVE IN BLOOM SERIES

SNOW SISTERS

Sisters in Love
Sisters in Bloom
Sisters in White

THE BRADENS at Weston

Lovers at Heart, Reimagined
Destined for Love
Friendship on Fire
Sea of Love
Bursting with Love
Hearts at Play

THE BRADENS at Trusty

Taken by Love
Fated for Love
Romancing My Love
Flirting with Love
Dreaming of Love
Crashing into Love

THE BRADENS at Peaceful Harbor

Healed by Love
Surrender My Love
River of Love
Crushing on Love
Whisper of Love
Thrill of Love

THE BRADENS & MONTGOMERYS at Pleasant Hill – Oak Falls

Embracing Her Heart
Anything For Love
Trails of Love
Wild, Crazy Hearts
Making You Mine
Searching For Love
Hot For Love

THE BRADEN NOVELLAS

Promise My Love
Our New Love
Daring Her Love
Story of Love
Love at Last
A Very Braden Christmas

THE REMINGTONS

Game of Love
Stroke of Love
Flames of Love
Slope of Love
Read, Write, Love
Touched by Love

SEASIDE SUMMERS

Seaside Dreams
Seaside Hearts
Seaside Sunsets
Seaside Secrets
Seaside Nights
Seaside Embrace

Seaside Lovers
Seaside Whispers
Seaside Serenade

BAYSIDE SUMMERS

Bayside Desires
Bayside Passions
Bayside Heat
Bayside Escape
Bayside Romance
Bayside Fantasies

THE STEELES AT SILVER ISLAND

Tempted by Love
My True Love
Always Her Love
Enticing Her Love
Caught by Love
Wild Island Love

THE RYDERS

Seized by Love
Claimed by Love
Chased by Love
Rescued by Love
Swept Into Love

THE WHISKEYS: DARK KNIGHTS AT PEACEFUL HARBOR

Tru Blue
Truly, Madly, Whiskey
Driving Whiskey Wild
Wicked Whiskey Love

Mad About Moon
Taming My Whiskey
The Gritty Truth
Running On Diesel
In For A Penny

SUGAR LAKE
The Real Thing
Only for You
Love Like Ours
Finding My Girl

HARMONY POINTE
Call Her Mine
This is Love
She Loves Me

THE WICKEDS: DARK KNIGHTS AT BAYSIDE
A Little Bit Wicked
The Wicked Aftermath

WILD BOYS AFTER DARK
Logan
Heath
Jackson
Cooper

BAD BOYS AFTER DARK
Mick
Dylan
Carson
Brett

HARBORSIDE NIGHTS SERIES

Includes characters from the Love in Bloom series

Catching Cassidy

Discovering Delilah

Tempting Tristan

More Books by Melissa

Chasing Amanda (mystery/suspense)

Come Back to Me (mystery/suspense)

Have No Shame (historical fiction/romance)

Love, Lies & Mystery (3-book bundle)

Megan's Way (literary fiction)

Traces of Kara (psychological thriller)

Where Petals Fall (suspense)

Acknowledgments

I hope you enjoyed Penny and Scott's story as much as I loved writing it. You can thank my close friend Lisa Filipe for pushing me into writing this story now, rather than later, and for reminding me how important it is to listen to my characters and to squeeze their stories into my already jam-packed schedule before I lose their voices. Sleep is overrated, right? Thank you, Lisa, for being just as nutty as I am.

I'm looking forward to bringing you many more Whiskey love stories, including the upcoming Colorado Whiskeys at Redemption Ranch, whom you can meet in *Searching for Love*, a Bradens & Montgomerys novel.

If you'd like to find out more about my writing process, get sneak peeks into stories and characters, and chat with me, please join my fan club on Facebook.
www.facebook.com/groups/MelissaFosterFans

Follow my author pages on Facebook and Instagram for fun giveaways and updates of what's going on in our fictional boyfriends' worlds.
www.facebook.com/MelissaFosterAuthor
www.instagram.com/melissafoster_author

If you prefer sweet romance, with no explicit scenes or graphic language, please try the Sweet with Heat series written under my pen name, Addison Cole. You'll find the many great love stories with toned-down heat levels.

Thank you to my meticulous editorial team, Kristen Weber and Penina Lopez, and my thorough proofreaders, Elaini Caruso, Juliette Hill, Marlene Engel, Lynn Mullan, and Justinn Harrison. And as always, thank you to my family for your endless support and allowing me time to disappear into my fictional worlds.

Meet Melissa

www.MelissaFoster.com

Melissa Foster is a *New York Times* and *USA Today* bestselling and award-winning author. Her books have been recommended by *USA Today*'s book blog, *Hagerstown* magazine, *The Patriot*, and several other print venues. Melissa has painted and donated several murals to the Hospital for Sick Children in Washington, DC.

Visit Melissa on her website or chat with her on social media. Melissa enjoys discussing her books with book clubs and reader groups and welcomes an invitation to your event. Melissa's books are available through most online retailers in paperback and digital formats.

Melissa also writes sweet romance under the pen name Addison Cole.

Free Reader Goodies: www.MelissaFoster.com/Reader-Goodies